The Guitar Player

and Other
Songs of Exile

The Guitar Player

and Other Songs of Exile

Jo Ann Kiser

atmosphere press

To Ezra and Hazel Kiser, my parents,
who are deeply missed

CONTENTS

The Guitar Player	3
Daughters	29
The Wedding Ring Quilt	41
Cresco	59
Paradise	71
Tecumseh	85
Mortlake Terrace	115
A Subversive	129
Sunday Afternoons	147
Going Home	163
His Story	173
Decoration Day	183
Blackberry Picking	191
Encounters of a Close Kind	199

The Guitar Player

It is always summer as Clara sits on the gate's wooden frame and hooks her feet in its wire-taut webbing. Locusts give their thin high wail in the dust, and in the left corner of the yard hollyhocks are blooming, pink and purple and white. Beyond them the garden begins with a jumble of cucumber vines, then rows of potatoes, beans, tomatoes, peppers, okra, melons, corn, cushaws, onions, radishes, the frame bed of lettuce, cabbages, carrots, mustard, and in the sandy patch near the creek sweet potatoes. There is a time to come when she will be far away and sometimes hungry, and at night she will close her eyes and walk through the garden.

The gray house has been moved now to make way for a strip-mining access road.

It is always summer, and on the blacktop county road, Hollis Ray swings himself down from the back of the rusty pickup truck and slings his guitar strap over his shoulder. Tall, his pale hair ashine, he walks by and as he passes Clara says, "Howdy, Hollis Ray," and he nods his head and says, "Howdy there."

"Why don't he talk?" Clara asks as her mother flicks her finger on the hot iron, testing.

"I reckon it was Vietnam. Go pick me some lettuce for supper."

Clara's father plays music too. He plays by ear. When he comes across an instrument, he softly worries it like a dog with a delectable bone until he brings forth tuneful sounds. Later on, in their wanderings, they will live in a brown house that has an old piano in one room. Otis, who has found work in a steel mill, shuts himself up in that room and plays for hours: "Wildwood Flower," "Barbry Allen," "Pretty Polly." One old song contains the words "I am a man of constant sorrow."

By that time, Clara understands that music to her father is a solitary meditation. He often accompanies his music with a pleasant, if choppy, baritone, and as she grows older, she listens to his voice and wonders about all the things in his world that she does not know. Instinctively she feels that these have been hurtful things, and she shrinks from the music he makes, from the things from which he has protected her, as she had shrunk earlier from the Old Regular Baptist hymns, their mournful unsparing chant.

But when Clara is six, Hollis Ray's guitar makes rich sounds of promise. Life will forever be within the green circle of the hills, and she will grow up to resemble her mother, with long black plaits of hair coroneted about her head. Her parents keep their secrets well. What does she know of the dank, low-ceilinged mine where Otis crawls, of Minnie's two miscarriages which preceded her own birth?

What is this war that has silenced Hollis Ray? Her uncle, too, had come back from it, but he never talked about it, though Mamaw showed them a color photograph of Uncle Eddie with a Vietnamese girl.

It is Clara's first year of school. The schoolhouse stands at the other end of the dirt road, and far up the mountain above it, she can see Hollis Ray's house. In the three years she attends the school, she sees him pass only two or three times, at noon, while she was eating a bologna and mustard sandwich, perhaps, or playing tag with her best friend Kate, or watching small Jonas eat his quart jarful of cornbread and milk down to the last mushy bite.

Owing to the efforts of the teacher, who had gone away to college in Ohio, the school is becoming a community center, and on Saturday nights, there are movies. As Clara approaches that magical night world, a parent holding either hand, she lifts her head in safety and sees the pure white light in Hollis Ray's windows, minute and distant, obscured by wind-tossed leaves. He lives there with his uncle Pete. His father was killed in a slate fall at the mine when he was ten, and his mother died of pneumonia while he was gone to war. Clara thinks the silent young man must at least talk to his uncle Pete. But yet he exists for her in solitariness, promising, like the light of his window, something that echoes his music and, at the same time, more faintly, her distant womanhood. (Or is it only in her memory, the grown Clara wonders, a memory tempered by their separate futures, that he existed so poignantly, that reserved tall youth with the deep, sweet dark-blue eyes striding past the gate in his loose country way with his guitar slung over his shoulder?)

5

They drive out of Columbus amid snow flurries, but south of Lexington, spring has come. On the hills sarvis bushes bloom white and redbuds gleam amid the gesturing trees.

The road swings around Sarvis Mountain, and from high up, she finds herself staring down at the old one-room schoolhouse where she had stood up in the primer class and talked aloud until the teacher told her to sit down and be quiet. Now the children go to a consolidated school several miles away. At the side of the road a white-haired man sits in front of his shabby house and plays a guitar.

"There's Hollis Ray," she says excitedly.

"You sure you want to do this," Alec asks as they slow down. "How many years has it been since you saw him?"

In the car with its closed windows, she cannot hear the music. "Pull over, Alec."

He shunts the car onto a gravel shoulder just past the house, turns off the engine, and lets down his window. Strains of "The Girl in the Blue Velvet Band" (*and now, folks, here's Bill Monroe and his Bluegrass Boys*). Chords and variations. "He's good," Alec pontificates.

The music ceases. Hollis Ray comes over to the car on Alec's side. He is wearing old jeans and a thin plaid shirt with a torn pocket.

"Are you Hollis Ray? Hollis Ray Danvers?" she asks eagerly.

He leans over and peers in at her. "Yes, ma'am."

"I'm Otis Fenton's oldest girl," she says.

"Clarrie," he says. "Clarrie Fenton?"

"It's been a long time." She holds out her hand to touch the past. "How are you, Hollis Ray?"

"I been good," he tells her. "A whole lot better 'n I was in Columbus. How's your daddy?"

"Daddy died, about ten years ago." She puts her hand on

Alec's shoulder. "This is my husband, Alec."

"You play that guitar like a pro," Alec says.

"Thanks," Hollis Ray replies awkwardly. "You come to visit, I guess."

"The Corlisses are having their family reunion like we do every year," Clara tells him. "We dropped by, hoping you'd come over and maybe play us a song or two. Would you, Hollis Ray?"

"Always glad to strum a little," he says. "You can count on me."

"It's been a long time," she repeats.

"Could I hitch me a ride down the hill and over to Pardo's grocery? It's on your way, or I wouldn't ask."

"Climb right in," Alec says, unlocking the back door.

"My cousin Alma told me you been back a long time," she says as Alec creeps cautiously around a steep curve. Her locution is half-willed, half-inevitable.

"I come on back home about twelve years ago when my uncle died and left me the house."

"Was that your mother's brother Pete?"

"Yeah. He never did get married. Like me, I reckon. Too damn lazy to go courting."

She remembers a time when Hollis Ray never talked casually, never joked.

"Did you stay in Columbus long after we moved away?"

"Oh, I stayed a *long* time," he replies somberly, looking out the window. "There's Pardo's."

Alec draws up in front of the small grocery store with the Dr. Pepper sign on the porch. It has probably once been a house. Whose? she wonders, but she can't remember. An old man is sitting on the porch edge chewing tobacco, and she finds his face familiar, but she isn't sure.

"Well, I'll see you folks tomorrow," Hollis Ray says as he

7

gets out.

"Howdy, folks," the old man greets them.

"Howdy," Alec replies and grins at her.

"You folks got people around here?"

"Yes," she says eagerly. "You know the Fentons? Or the Corlisses?"

"Lord, yes," he exclaims. "Jarvey Corliss was my buddy in the Big Creek mine."

"That's my uncle," she informs Alec, but he is intent on returning to the road. She waves frantically backward.

Alec is Clara's second husband, and this is his first time in the hills. Clara met him, a widower, while researching an article for the *Columbus Dispatch* on an upscale theater group. She closely watched when she introduced him to her mother, who still kept a Kentucky accent and wore her mountain past wrapped around her like a winter coat. But she need not have worried. "I could have done worse," she congratulated herself. Sometimes, though, on awakening in the night, Clara feels some great event in her head, a rush of imminence like an impending heart attack or a sudden psychosis. She sits up in bed and cries silently for the barefoot child who does not recognize the stranger who sleeps beside her.

After leaving Pardo's and getting lost twice, Alec and Clara find the dirt road where Alma and her family live. The rented car chugs steeply up the grade. Young green leaves flutter against the windows. "What happens if you meet someone who's going down?" Alec asks.

"Somebody's got to back up."

"My god."

"There," she points, and they turn abruptly left and climb sharply into Alma's backyard, under the giant hickory, behind a pickup, a battered Ford, and her mother's new Saturn.

Alma, her plump body relaxed in a cotton house dress but her gray hair stiff from the beauty salon, opens the screen door. "Howdy, folks. Come on in and take a load off your feet." Her husband, Breece, big and bald, is standing beside Alma, who says, "Your mom's resting. That long trip tuckered her out."

Clara introduces everyone to Alec, who smiles and says, "What a beautiful place you have here."

"Well. It's home," Breece answers laconically. The living room stands on stilts and looks down, down over the mountains, over the green and over the white sarvis, and the redbuds clustering. At a distant gap, the sky sits like a bird with blue wings poised.

A small hand tugs at Clara's coat. "I got me a pet rabbit." Clara accepts the hand of Alma's grandson and goes out to the rabbit hutch. Beyond it, a small patch of flat land has already been plowed, and the lettuce bed has been made up and planted, but the onion sets haven't been put out yet. This knowledge comes back to Clara intimately, strongly.

When she returns to the house, her mother is in the kitchen sipping coffee and talking to Alma. Clara searches her broad, sweet face, its brown eyes, for signs of wear. Looking up and seeing Clara, Mrs. Corliss absentmindedly smiles and turns back to Alma. It comes once more to Clara that her mother is a woman of split allegiances.

Coming in from the hall, where he has been talking to Breece about cars and the weather, Alec takes Clara's hand and separates her even further from the intimate scene between the two other women.

It is noon in Columbus. Clara is a scholarship student at Ohio State. It is a Sunday, and she has been walking, walking, walking. She is walking down a seedy street (a geranium blooming suddenly red on a crumbling windowsill). Out of the shabby, neon-lit bar wobbles a man who looks like Hollis Ray Danvers. He is wearing patched blue jeans and a faded cotton shirt with stains on it. He smells, and his face is stiff with bone. Without even thinking, she says, "Howdy, Hollis Ray," but the man doesn't appear to hear her. She follows him. Grimy children are playing marbles on the sidewalk, and a mangy yellow dog flops down in a tiny yard with sunburnt grass. Women with badly permed hair look at her as they hang clothes out on back porches. The man who resembles Hollis Ray goes into a building that says, simply, "Hotel." Clara looks inside. It is dark in there, and the carpet is threadbare and dirty. The man goes past the desk clerk without speaking and in the silence climbs the creaking stairs. Scared and faintly nauseous, Clara hurries away. It has been almost a decade since Clara last saw Hollis Ray, a week before her family left Sarvis Creek. She had just entered the fifth grade when Otis got laid off at the mine.

They moved first to Florida, Otis's dream state to which he had once hopped a freight in his youth. Sometimes after a drink of Southern Comfort he would talk about sunshine and ocean and oranges growing. But he had found only temporary work in Florida. After a year, they moved to North Carolina, then to West Virginia, and, when the mines went bust again, to Ohio, where for a while he had a job in a factory. She remembers beans and cornbread for breakfast and for supper too. She remembers kids calling them hillbillies. Otis grew silent, and Minnie talked softly to her oldest daughter of home. Clara does not really want to talk to the familiar-looking drunk. She returns to the warm college dorm and forgets about him.

In December, she takes a Greyhound to the small town near which her family now lives. They have fallen on hard times again. Otis is working part-time repairing barges that run on the Ohio River. When he pulls up at the bus station in the battered old Chevy, Clara is shocked by the lines on her father's forehead.

A cedar tree has been chopped down in the snowy wood behind the house, brought in and decorated with familiar shining ornaments, and at the top, a cardboard star covered with aluminum foil. Her mother holds out her arms. Her brothers and sisters tease her. She is not fully aware that the appliance store in town has reclaimed the electric stove and that Minnie is cooking on the old coal stove they have lugged from place to place. Nor that the Santa gifts for the younger ones are meager. They have been sending her five dollars a month for spending money.

It is not that Clara doesn't say sharply, "How mean can you get?" about the appliance store, or that she doesn't listen to Minnie's woes whispered, as always, beyond Otis's earshot. It is not that she doesn't feel a momentarily keen sympathy for the children. But she is not really there. She has secretly divorced herself from them and joined a world where food and lodging and daily comfort are thoughtlessly accepted.

Christmas night, when she comes downstairs in the drafty house, Minnie cries as they drag out the cardboard box of cheap presents, and Otis slumps into a chair and buries his face in his hands. He looks up at Clara and blurts out, "You're goin' to have to drop out of school." She says out of panic, without thought, "No, no, I won't," but her mother says, "Hush," and hugs her while her father's face tightens with shame. He has been laid off. Silently they fill the socks with Milky Ways and Juicy Fruit, and English walnuts.

Clara spends Christmas Day in the room that she shares with a sister, who is downstairs helping Minnie get Christmas dinner. No one yells at Clara to come down. Minnie has warned them off. They have been warned off Otis, too, who is as silent as his eldest daughter. When dinner is ready, her sister Annie knocks politely at the door.

In mid-January, Otis and Clara and Luke crowd into the pickup cab. Otis's cardboard suitcase and the blue plastic one they had bought Clara for college and two brown paper bags (one containing their lunch of bologna sandwiches and apples and a thermos of coffee and a Pepsi for Luke) sit in the truck bed under a tarpaulin. They set off in the dirty snow left over from Christmas. Otis and Clara are still silent. Luke, his eager face peering through the windshield as they head north, is fifteen, and this is his first stay away from home. Clara is dreading their arrival at Ohio State, where she must go to the dorm and remove her belongings and say goodbye to her college acquaintances.

She gets through it, of course, and comes downstairs with the final blue plastic suitcase and the purple turtle her roommate had given her on her birthday. Without a word, Otis stores the suitcase under the tarpaulin, and she follows suit with the turtle while curious students look from the steps. "They'll let you come back, won't they?" he asks as he starts the truck up.

"I don't know."

He drives carefully through the thickening evening traffic. "You'll be back," he says.

Otis takes Clara and Luke to a place somewhere east on Broad Street, where the brick houses are crumbling and the people are poorly dressed. There is a bar on one corner and a mean-looking hotel on another. Their landlady rents out her second floor—two rooms on one side of the hall and two rooms on the other. Both sides share the bathroom.

The woman who leads the way up the cracked wooden stair has legs swollen with thick blue veins. Clara sees the iron-gray roots of her thin brown hair. She has a damp, sick smell, or is it the house? The upper hallway is covered with patched brown linoleum. "There ain't nobody living across the hall," she tells Otis. "You fellers'll have the bathroom all to yourself."

Clara lifts the dirty curtain drawn across the doorway into the other room. Another lumpy mattress and a box with a cracked mirror above it. "That's your room," Otis says. They go down and bring up her college stuff and shove it under the bed and in the closet.

There is no refrigerator. Otis goes out in the morning and gets some instant coffee. Minnie has packed them a box of cereal, along with a box of dried milk and a jar of peanut butter. She has also packed two kettles, and Otis heats water for the coffee on the hotplate. He has bought the *Columbus Dispatch*. After he looks through the want ads, he passes them on to Clara.

Clara finds an employment agency that advertises "Openings in advertising and publishing." It has a down-town address near the expensive department store where she had gone with her college roommates. In the next two weeks, they anxiously conserve Otis's money from unemployment checks—most of it goes to the family at home. At the employment agency, the blonde woman who wears suits and starched blouses sends Clara, who is an excellent typist, on several interviews at advertising and public relations firms, at law firms and engineering firms. They praise her spelling and typing, but none of them hire her.

On the second Friday, the agency woman looks at Clara and says, "There's a job you're just right for. An editorial assistant job at a textbook publisher. Go buy a good navy blue dress and some hosiery."

"I don't think I can," Clara answers stiffly.

"You must if you want a job that uses your skills."

So Clara goes back to the linoleum-floored rooms with the scarred furniture and the bathroom across the hall and tells her father, who has spent all day looking for a job and who has had no lunch and who now sits despondently at the graffiti-laden table, that she needs a "good" navy blue dress.

"And that'll get you the job?"

"I don't know, Daddy."

"I got next month's rent squirreled away. If you have to, you have to."

In the morning, Clara goes to an expensive women's clothing store and buys a blue dress with white piping and a pair of hose, and then she walks to the agency. "Change in here," the blonde woman says and shows her into the staff bathroom. When she has changed, she puts her hair in a French twist, as she has learned to do at Ohio State, and applies pink drugstore lipstick.

"Good girl," the woman says. "Those shoes aren't too bad." And Clara goes off to be interviewed by the editor who is in need of an assistant. From the way he treats her, she knows that she must at least look the part, and he is pleased with her skills. Two days later, the woman at the agency tells her, when she calls from the pay phone in front of the bar, that the job is hers.

She goes back to the rooms with their linoleum floors and says excitedly to Luke (Otis is out job hunting), "I got the job."

"Can we go home for a visit now?" he asks. Otis has

forbidden Luke to go into the streets without him or Clara, and Clara's brother spends long aimless hours in the front room, reading the westerns that Otis has brought from home and Clara's *1984* and *Wuthering Heights*. He looks pale and unhappy. Suddenly Clara sees him. "I don't know. We'll ask Daddy."

Otis returns around six, sits down on the bed, and props his feet on a chair. "Bring me a glass of water," he tells Luke.

"Clara got a job."

"For a publisher of books," Clara says. "A pretty good job."

"How much?"

"Ninety a week."

He lets out a long sigh. "I'm glad one of us got one," he says and pauses. "You gonna like it?"

"It's all right," she answers half-grudgingly, half-excitedly. "Can we go home this weekend?"

"Not 'til you get your first paycheck, honey." Only once in a long while does Otis call his girl children honey. "Maybe I'll have a job by then. Though it don't look like it, it don't look like it." Clara has discovered in the last few weeks that their father repeats himself when he is unhappy.

Otis goes out one evening and comes back at eleven with sour breath. Clara and Luke are sitting in the larger room reading. They no longer seem to have anything to say to each other. "Guess who I ran into," Otis says. "Hollis Ray Danvers. I don't know if you remember him, Clara. He used to play guitar on the radio."

"I think I saw him once back during the spring. I forgot to tell you."

"You stay away from him," Otis says, turning to look at her more closely.

"Why? Because he's a drunk now?"

"No, he's not a drunk no more. How come you know he was drinking a lot?"

"Because the man I saw was drunk."

"Well, Hollis don't drink at all now."

"Then how come we can't talk to him?"

"I didn't say you couldn't say hello if you was to pass him by."

"Do I have to stay away from him too?" Luke asks.

"It's not the same," Otis says. "You're a boy."

Clara's cheeks burn at the idea of her father thinking about her and men. She wants to talk about Hollis Ray on Sarvis Creek, about being six and sitting on the gate. A gust of love for her father, for Luke, for the family shakes her like a sapling before the storm. She looks at her father and sees his fear for her, his despair and loneliness. "I miss Sarvis Creek," she says.

"Aaaaaah, it ain't no use crying over spilt milk," he replies heavily.

"I don't remember Sarvis Creek," Luke says, looking at both of them distrustfully. "When we goin' home?"

"I get a paycheck next week," Clara says. She wants to see her mother and the others, to sit lonely under a tree and feel the breeze and the sun like emissaries from God sweeping her mind clean.

Otis rubs Luke's head. "Next weekend, then," he says. "We'll go home next weekend."

Clara likes her boss. He looks like a well-toned teddy bear and has short, crisp hair, almost a crewcut. There is a picture of his family on his desk, warm and well-fed and beaming, with the prettiness of smooth skin and shining hair. His wife must be about Minnie's age, but with her blonde hair, her lipstick, and her trim figure, she looks much younger to Clara's untrained eye. On Friday, after

Clara receives her paycheck, Otis and Luke come to get her so that they can go directly home.

"Who's that Goliath?" John, the head designer, asks, looking out the window. "And David's with him."

Clara pretends not to hear as she makes her way to the front door.

They cash her check at a place that charges a fee. Otis clucks his tongue. "Can't help it this time," he says. "I got to keep this money, Clara. I got to keep it all this time."

"Yeah," she answers, fighting down her resentment, her wish to finger the money, to go to an expensive store and buy a silk dress like the one Janice had worn yesterday, to get her hair done and flirt with John.

Otis looks at her and then hands her five dollars. "You ought to get *somethin'* out of your first paycheck," he says.

They don't stop for supper but pull in by the house about nine o'clock. Light spills out of the windows, and people spill onto the porch, the tender welcome of her mother and the excited voices of Annie and Jennie and Jacob. Otis has bought some orange gumdrops (Minnie's favorite) at the little store where he got gas, and he hands them to Minnie, who takes one and doles the rest out to the children, which includes not only Luke but also Clara. Like homecoming pilgrims after a long and weary journey, they enter the house to the fried chicken (Minnie has killed the last of the fryers) and gravy and cornbread. When Clara crumbles cornbread into her chicken gravy, she wonders what Yvonne and Janice would think.

As she had done before she went away to school, she reads a story to Jennie, with Annie and Jacob listening too, although they can read perfectly well by themselves now. Luke hangs by his father's side, the two of them going out with a lantern to look at the cow, at the garden, at everything.

Clara goes to bed like a small child, the low murmur of her parents' voices barely heard from the main bedroom.

The next week Otis gets a job doing electrical work in an air-conditioning factory. It is a few miles out of town, and he says he can't wait until they can move out of town and bring Minnie and the children up. Luke's face lights up.

Clara had been taking art appreciation at school, and when Saturday comes, she asks Otis if she and Luke can go to the art museum.

"Art museum? Well, I guess so, long as Luke's with you. Where is it?"

They walk the miles to the museum. Clara has made peanut butter sandwiches, and on the way, they stop in a small restaurant and order a Coke apiece.

Clara stands entranced before a Cezanne. A hidden order charges that landscape, boundaries that keep the abyss at bay.

Soon she has to go looking for Luke. She finds him before a painting of two horses, their colors strong against a dark background.

"You like it?" she asks.

"It's okay, I guess," he says, stepping away and looking at the floor.

They are almost back to their rooms when they pass Hollis Ray on the street. He doesn't see them. He is talking to an old man who has a grizzled beard and wears a pair of patched overalls. The man is smoking a rough-looking pipe.

"Did you see that old man?" she whispers to Luke. "He had a corncob pipe."

"Ah. There ain't no such thing," Luke says suspiciously.

"Yes, there is, too. Great-aunt Dulcy smokes one."

When they get to the rooms, Otis is lying on the bed

reading a Max Brand western. "Daddy," Luke asks, "is there such a thing as a corncob pipe?"

"Lord, yes. How come you're asking?"

"I thought Clara was pulling my leg."

"It's an old thing, son. Just a few people up the hollers still smoke a corncob pipe."

"Will you show me how to make one?"

"After we get us another farm and raise some more corn."

Luke goes down the hall to the bathroom, and Otis says to Clara, "The young ones don't know nothing about Sarvis Creek."

"We saw Hollis Ray out on the street," she tells her father. "He was with a man who was smoking a corncob pipe."

"Now, maybe that's his uncle Pete," Otis replies with interest. "He said he was coming up sometime soon. I wouldn't mind passing the time of day with him." He gets off the bed and ties his shoes. "Reckon I'll go down and see if it's him. You and Luke go ahead and eat supper."

They eat their Campbell's tomato soup and bologna sandwiches and wonder what is keeping him so long.

They don't go home again during the next month because Otis is saving all the money he can from both their paychecks. They are going to rent a house in about two months, and bring up the rest of the family. Cramped in the two scarred rooms, the three of them grow tired of each other. Otis lets Clara and Luke go walking downtown, but they have hardly anything to spend. They fight over whether to take the bus home (Clara) or have a chocolate milkshake (Luke). They go back to the art museum, which is free. They find a public library, finally, and borrow a stack of books.

So Clara stays in the tiny room and reads Jane Austen, all of Jane Austen. She thinks despairingly in her moments alone when she puts down a book that she is too messy, that she never will attain such order and beauty. She is doomed, and her reawakened love for her family is part of that doom. She takes little joy in the mostly secretarial work she performs at the publisher's, and the textbooks they publish are too abstruse for her story-oriented mind to take any great interest in. She is troubled by, on the one hand, the fact that Janice and Yvonne and John and her boss seem to accept her as one of them, when she knows she is not, and on the other hand, by the distance between her and all of them, by the easy way in which they chat with each other, by the stories they have in common. They talk, for example, about going to camp in the summer when they were young.

On Saturday night, Otis says, "I'm going to meet Hollis Ray." For two weeks, he hasn't done anything but work and come back to the rooms, except for a walk on Sundays with Clara and Luke. He is working a six-day week.

"Can I come too?" Luke asks.

"No, you stay here with your sister."

"I'll come too," Clara says.

"A bar's no place for you," Otis says.

It is a warm spring evening. If Clara looks out of the single window in her room, she can see a small tree growing in a back lot, a tree of green embers which a breeze seems about to fan into flame. It speaks of order and beauty, a bare hint adrift in the growing dark.

"Clarrie, come here," Luke calls. He is staring out of the window. "It's Daddy," he says. "He's fighting some guys."

Without thinking, she is out the door and down the stairs, Luke right behind her.

"Stay back," a voice sasses at them. "I said stay back." It

is Hollis Ray, who passes them, clenching his fists. She sees blood spurt from her father's nostril and actually reaches out her hand to clutch the enemy's shirtsleeve, but from among the growing crowd of men, another hand pulls hers back, and she sees that someone is holding Luke.

Hollis Ray and her father win out. The hands let go of her and Luke, and they run to Otis, who is holding his head. He has a deep cut on his cheek and neck, and there is blood all over his shirt.

"Now, Luke, get on his other side," Hollis Ray says, "and Clara, you open the doors. We got to get him out of here before the police come."

Clara feels sick. She opens the doors, and they lead Otis, limping and groggy, up to the linoleum-floored rooms. "He cut you," Hollis Ray says.

"Yeah. Looked like a paring knife."

"It's pretty deep on your throat. We better get you to a doctor."

"Can't afford it."

Clara says, "You got to, Daddy. It might get infected. You got to."

"Yeah," Luke adds anxiously. "You got to."

"See there now," Hollis Ray says. "These kids know. We'll clean you up a little, and I'll take you over to the emergency room. I know a doc there won't call the police. Him and me used to be drinking buddies. Difference is, I quit and he didn't."

Otis groans. "I got to go to work Monday," he says. "I got to."

"You sure can't do that. I'll call up Monday morning and tell them you got hurt."

"Tell 'em I got in a fight?" Otis asks.

The two men look at each other. "No, I reckon not,"

Hollis Ray answers. "I'll tell 'em some men jumped you and took your wallet and left you lying there."

"Okay," Otis says heavily and turns his face to the wall.

"He's got to rest," Hollis Ray whispers. "Doc said to feed him light tomorrow."

Soft-boiled eggs and mashed potatoes and toast—that is all Clara can think of. And soup. In the morning, while Otis is sleeping, she takes some dollar bills from his wallet and sends Luke out to get eggs and some Campbell's mushroom soup. They have brought potatoes back from home, a large paper bag full of them. The potatoes sit in a dark corner and grow sprouts, sending an earthy smell through the rooms.

Someone knocks while Otis is eating his egg and toast breakfast. Clara opens the door and sees Hollis Ray's lean face, now with a large bruise to the side of his right eye, half-hidden by his fair hair. Otis, unshaven and gaunt above his bandaged throat, says, "Come on in, partner."

"I'm going to be here talkin' to your daddy," Hollis Ray says awkwardly to Luke, "if you and your sister want to get out for a while."

They walk silently over to Broad Street and down to where the tall buildings are. "You think Daddy's goin' to be all right," Luke asks anxiously.

"Yep," Clara says heartily, worrying about whether or not their father will lose the job. They wander aimlessly downtown, not having enough money left to spend on anything. It's getting dark by the time they turn onto their street, and when they get upstairs, Otis and Hollis Ray are still talking.

Between spoonfuls of mushroom soup, Otis tells Clara, "It'll be all right about the job. They told Hollis Ray to tell me it'd be all right long as I got there by Thursday." Clara nods unsurely. "Soon as I get paid next Friday, we'll start looking for a house. Time I got you two out of here."

"And you too," Luke says, looking teasingly at his father, lying under Minnie's bright log-cabin quilt, which shines red and gold in the dark room.

Otis laughs. "And me too."

And Clara feels that for the moment, it is all right.

On Friday night, Otis gets his paycheck, and on his way home, he collects big, juicy hamburgers from a truck stop near where he works and some cold bottles of Pepsi, and Hollis Ray and his guitar. "Tomorrow," he says, smiling, "we start looking for a house."

"Hallelujah," Luke shouts.

"Sshhh. We don't want to get throwed out before we're ready to leave."

As they munch on the hamburgers, Clara finds herself looking at the way Hollis Ray's shoulders fit into his long back, at the way his eyes shine darkly out. Once or twice he looks over at her, the blue shining directly at her. He plays "Wildwood Flower," and "Barbry Allen," and "Your Cheating Heart," "Red River Valley," and the "Great Speckled Bird." He plays on and on, guitar sound shivering against the night windows and falling back into the room, falling into Clara's heart, into the aperture that had closed when they left Sarvis Creek, like silver pebbles falling into a well.

"Well, I thank you for that," Otis says at midnight, and Hollis gets up quietly and leaves them.

They find a house quickly, an old two-story frame house about thirty miles outside Columbus, with a solid barn, a large garden, and a cornfield. Clara's new bedroom faces east, and in the mornings, the sun rises like a promise. Evenings she works in the garden alongside Annie and Jennifer (Luke and Jacob help Mr. Radaker, their farmer-landlord, plow and plant), making up potato ridges and dropping seed corn. Minnie sings as she hangs new curtains in the kitchen.

One Saturday, Clara asks her father to drive her to the bus station, as he does on workdays, so that she can spend a day in Columbus going to a movie, having lunch out, wearing the new copper-colored silk dress she bought with the paycheck which Otis told her to keep for herself. Someone steals her wallet out of her bag while she is watching the Paul Newman movie. All she has left is a little change in the bottom of the bag. There is no telephone at home. Standing on a side street into which she has wandered, she thinks feverishly. The best she can do is to call Hollis Ray's hotel and hope he is at home.

She waits long minutes, imagining the dark hallway and shabby rooms, while they call him to the desk phone. She had hoped he would say he would meet her downtown, but he asks, "You got enough money to get here?" On the city bus, which takes all but a penny of her remaining change, she remembers her six-year-old self sitting on the garden gate and greeting Hollis Ray.

The desk clerk in the dark hotel leers at her and says, "Go on up, buttercup." She stands blushing in the doorway. His room is clean and sparse: a bed with a tightly tucked brown blanket, a wooden box for a nightstand, a skew-legged green chair. On the wall, he has taped a photograph of green hills torn from a magazine. He says, "Come on in for a minute." She thinks of him sitting alone in this little room when he comes home from work.

The guitar is propped against the wall. She asks him to play her a tune. He plays several. "Carry me back to old Virginny." He puts the guitar down and starts to come closer, his eyes like dark blue arrows. She hopes that he might kiss her, and when he does not, she looks at him with teary eyes. His lips are solid and warm, and she melts into his body, which is intimate and assured. After a few minutes of this, she is shaken by a desire to have his baby. Probably because of her role as the oldest daughter in a large family, Clara is not a girl who dreams of having children; in her romantic fantasies, she has never wanted a child. They do not make love. He draws apart from her and says, "I'm a friend of your daddy's. I can't do this." Alternately deprived and relieved, she doesn't know how to answer but awkwardly nods. He gets his wallet out and gives her money to get home, takes her downstairs, and sees her onto a bus.

At the end of the summer, Otis says at supper one night, "I reckon you can go back to school after Christmas if you want to." Knowing she will go, she cries that night until early morning. Minnie enters her room at dawn and holds her. "You sure you want to go, honey?"

The Corlisses have been holding their family reunions in the gymnasium at the Peach Fork Elementary School. On the white paper tablecloths sit rows of bowls and platters, kettles and pans, filled with home-cooked food whose smells sometimes war with each other. There is a separate table of homemade desserts, banana pudding, and 7-Up cake, among others. Clara has signed up as a possible recipient of the Came from the Longest Distance Award. Close to a hundred people mill about. Many of the older women have long hair pulled back in a bun and wear print dresses that fall below their knees. Children run busily among and around the adults. Clara keeps nudging her mother and whispering, "Who's that? Who's that?" The turn of a jaw, the slope of an eye, the shade of a head of hair:

as familiar as her own skin, but she cannot find a name.

Uncle August, her mother's oldest brother, who has a supermarket franchise in town, comes over and tells Clara, "I'm going to take this here husband of yours and introduce him to some good old country boys." Clara fills her plate with chicken and dumplings from a beat-up aluminum kettle and cornbread from a pan that has seen much use, and some lettuce salad from a beautiful large wooden bowl. As she rejoins her mother, she sees Alec and Hollis Ray.

"Look who I've found," Alec says. "With his guitar." The three of them wander outside together because Alec says he wants a breath of fresh air. He and Hollis Ray are talking about war. "I remember one time," Alec is saying, "walking by what was left of a guy who stepped on an IED. The thing that gets you most is the stench. There are certain smells even today that remind me of the war."

"I remember all them children walkin' around without parents, without anybody, and them wounded often as not, and no place to stay," Hollis Ray says. "I reckon we could've done without that war."

Beyond the flat, grassy yard back of the schoolhouse runs a clear mountain creek, tinted brown with sandstone pebbles and fringed on the far side with deep, soft moss. And beyond the moss, the hill rises gently, thick with ancient trees. "That there may be virgin timber," Hollis Ray points. "Some of the last around, if it is. Come on."

"My bum ankle is hurting. You two go ahead," Alec answers, leaning against the school gate. "I'll meet you back inside."

With an edge of illicit pleasure, Clara takes off her shoes to wade the creek. Hollis Ray merely strides across on a few precarious rocks.

"My hose are ruined," she says, looking down.

"You might as well leave them shoes off," Hollis Ray observes. "They ain't got much of a heel, but it's too much for this bank."

Her unaccustomed toes wrap themselves about root edges as her hands seek without direction holds on rocks, branches, roots. The earth that greets her is utterly familiar. They reach a mossy clearing. "I tried to bring one of them kids home," Hollis Ray is saying. "They called him Kim, but I think it was just because they didn't know his real name. He took up with me after I gave him some chocolate. A little thing like that."

"Do you ever regret coming back here?" she asks.

"Oh, I get an itchy foot once in a while but not really."

They fall silent. The afternoon sun shines its gold mist among the branches, onto the moss and the first violets. Clara remembers the child she was and Hollis Ray coming by with his guitar, saying hello. Soon they go back indoors and rejoin the others, and soon Clara and Alec leave for Ohio. It will be a long time before they head south again.

Daughters

There came to Opal early in life anxiety about naming things, so when she stood in her grandmother's hospital room, she looked at each device and told herself she must find out the name and purpose of it. Her mother stood by the bed, holding her own mother's hand. Opal's grandmother stirred and spoke, eyes still closed, calling Opal's mother "Sister," speaking a part in a seventy-year-old conversation, a child's game on a summer's day.

Opal had flown in from New York, leaving her husband of two years behind. She felt heavy with the child. She felt heavy with life, her New York self that until recently she had seemed to dwell in without consequences. Elemental to her thoughts these last few months had been the anticipation of her grandmother's holding Opal's child in the old cane-bottomed rocking chair where once she had held Opal, and before that Opal's mother, in the house beneath the hill, where the steep, tree-thick slope ran down to the clay path that ran along the flesh of the hill to the old swinging bridge over Sarvis Creek that led to her grandparents' house.

When Opal's family had lived in Ohio for several years, Mamaw came to make a lengthy visit. Papaw had died a decade ago, and she had taken to staying months at a time with each of her children. Now she was dying of cancer, and her serene good looks—echoed in Opal's mother's face—had been marred by many wrinkles. Her shoulders were bent, and her chest concave. Seeing her, Opal felt that old flesh settling about her own bones, as though she had robbed her grandmother of it, and she wondered if her mother also felt like a thief. Time's ravages were beginning to show in her mother's lovely face. It was framed by a black and gray coronet of braided hair—for Opal's mother had kept her Primitive Baptist looks if not the religion: paint-free face and long, long hair.

Opal's mother, Laurie, was a lean woman. The hard years had eroded those pleasant curves that leaned against Opal's father in that photograph taken shortly after their marriage in Mamaw's backyard below Sarvis Mountain. Their young figures stood tightly under a locust tree, frozen by Opal's eyes, while branches, leaves, vines on the fence looped, sprawled, curled, growing out of sight on every side.

When Opal and her mother returned from the hospital, the men went out and got a pizza. They also heated up some leftover vegetables in the microwave. After supper, Opal and her mother washed the few dishes, and while they were doing so, Opal told her mother the news that she had been withholding far too long.

Her mother said, "Well, I knew *that*," looked at Opal intensely, then disappeared into the master bedroom. Not knowing what to do, Opal joined her father and brother in the living room for an hour. Her mother did not reappear. Finally, Opal went to find her.

Already Opal was showing, despite her artfully chosen skirt. Opal was afraid. One of her earliest memories was of her mother, home after Matthew's birth, lying in bed with her legs bent across an upside-down chair so that the blood clot in her leg wouldn't move upward before the ambulance came. In the crib beside the bed, the baby had been crying.

Now the older woman was listening to the Grand Ole Opry. Yes, she was lean sitting there, doodling that telltale address, that name. Standing in the doorway, Opal saw that she had made herself oblivious, listening to those songs of passion and loss, doodling as always, "Laura Jean Fenton, Sarvis, Kentucky." Did she ever, the next morning, pick up the paper and see what memory had revealed? What starved creatures perched in those large gray eyes? They rested silently among newly etched wrinkles, looking beyond Opal.

Opal went to the bureau, took the shoebox of photographs from the bottom drawer, and went back into the living room where the men were talking. They had left the TV on but turned its volume down. Its images danced gray and black beyond the window. Grand Ole Opry sounds seeped through the wall from the bedroom.

Andrew, Opal's father, was reminiscing again. He sat in the shabby armchair with his shoulders permanently hunched, one eye askew from an old mining accident, knobby muscles disturbing his arms, one leg a little shorter because he got caught in a machine at the factory. He waved his arms, enveloping some old satisfaction.

Opal wondered if, after she blurted the news, her mother had gone to the bottom bureau drawer and, pulling out the photo box, reached beneath to feel the thing she kept there, that white blanket stained by yellow time? Her last-born, dead at birth. Her firstborn had died, too, and it had been touch and go with Opal's brother. Andrew had been out of work the year the last one died, right after the family moved to Ohio. The doctor reprimanded them for the lack of prenatal care.

"Well, I told Laurie to just keep quiet, and I took my gun and tiptoed out the back door. Sure enough, there them rascals were, right in the middle of our popcorn patch, a little the worse for Virgil's corn liquor, picking away. I slipped up a little closer and let out a yell, not letting on I know who they are. 'Who the goddamn hell's into my popcorn,' I said. 'Just let me get hold of you.' Well, they fetched up short and started sidling toward the other end. I lifted my gun and shot once, way over their heads. They run faster than I ever saw anybody run and I heard Henry, he was the oldest one, saying, 'Jim. Jim. Make legs, save body, Jim.'" When their father threw his head back in gusty laughter, Opal and her brother laughed, too. Opal had forgotten who Henry and Jim were.

I came out from the edge of the woods chasing a dragonfly. She looked across at me, from her perch on the top step, across the rising curve of her stomach, across the flower-spattered yard. She could not see the dragonfly, only my hands snapping at the air as I wheeled and turned, my tangled hair heavy with sunlight. The sun hung weightless over her head, frailflake suspended in rainwashed blue. She

was tired, though she hadn't worked in the garden because
of the thunderstorm. The baby was only a few weeks away.
Did she feel a sudden grace as she rested her arms on the
soft hill of her stomach, half-blinded perhaps by the way the
light broke on green blades of corn?

Still carrying the shoebox, Opal moved on into the kitchen, her mother's room. The living room was a TV sanctuary; Opal's room had become the spare room. Her brother, who now lived a few miles away, often came to spend the weekend, so he retained his bedroom. That would change soon. Matthew was engaged to a girl from Cleveland. Andrew dominated her parents' bedroom, pleasant dust of his pipes, his latest Western on the table, can of Prince Albert and socket, wire, or nails from his pockets on the dresser. Laurie kept only a Chapstick there. Her hand lotion was in the bathroom.

Opal sat down at the kitchen table and, putting the photographs aside, looked at the familiar room, inhaling some old peace. A messy cook, her mother made a great to-do of cleaning while she did the dishes. The battered pots sat gleaming on their shelves. The iron skillet (it had been Mamaw's) hung on its nail. Over the stove, a red rooster strutted on his yellow plaque. Laurie had made the curtains: a starched gold. In the far corner was the old churn; she stored her odds and ends there. On the shelf above the sink were her cookbooks and her recipe clippings pasted into a notebook. Her other books always found their way there, too. For years Opal and her mother had read the same books. Opal would bring them from the library, from school, and they would sail through them, sometimes acting out scenes, giggling as they improvised. Opal looked at the current collection. What did this woman take from books Opal had never read? She experienced a childish terror.

The older woman came into the kitchen carrying her empty coffee cup, not looking at Opal but busying herself at the stove. "You hungry? There's still some chicken in the refrigerator. Better take some before your daddy gets his hands on it."

"I'm not hungry, Mom." But then Opal spotted the old aluminum kettle sitting on a back cap. It was the same kettle that had sat at the back of the old coal stove when her mother had made pinto beans. She began to crave pinto bean soup, with cornbread unwrapped from its aluminum foil (her mother had used to keep it in a steep white breadbox, pink flowers, three of them, on the lid and a smooth black knob). Opal never cooked pinto beans herself.

While Opal slurped the soup, her mother picked up a book by Silas House and said, "Pretty good." Opal knew he was a new Kentucky writer and had been meaning to read him. Her mother started to add something but hesitated, uncertainty on her face. Opal answered weakly, "I haven't read it," and Laurie put the book back on the shelf.

Suddenly bereaved, Opal got up and opened the refrigerator, hiding her face in its frozen depths. The room was stained with light. *After Dr. Braceon said yes, you're going to have a baby, I left his office in a daze. Standing in the sun, I pulled out my cell phone to call Sam. Surrounded by students, he lowered his voice. Was he happy? Cars went down the street. Their engines grated. Traffic lights clacked their colors. Hands whirred on a clock.*

"Let's play some cards," she said to her mother. They took an ancient deck from a cupboard and sat down to five-stud poker. The two men came to join them. Opal bet too much, as she always did. "Look at this girl," her father said. "She don't even hold her cards right anymore."

After the card game, the others went to their beds.

Sleepless, Opal set up a game of solitaire. She placed the queen of hearts next to the king with her left hand and lay down the deck with her right, reaching her forefinger up to rub her temple and in the middle of the gesture recognized it as her grandmother's, her mother's. She had not felt ready to have a baby, but Sam had wanted one, and when it happened by accident, she had resigned herself. Already she worried about the birth and then about the child that she had to protect from all the bad things that might happen. She herself had led a protected life, but her parents, she knew, had not. Shuffling the cards, she remembered a story told to her by her father, not by her mother. Opal reckoned up the years and discovered that her mother had been two or three years younger than Opal was now.

Opal Elizabeth shifted in her cradle. Her daddy was coming back from town with potatoes—they had used the last of the ones in the smokehouse basement on Tuesday—and with strawberry jam for Sunday morning biscuits. Laurie Jean lifted the churn lid, folding back the white cloth beneath to see if the milk had turned. Her headaches and side aches and leg aches had faded now that Andy's cousin Ellie was there to do the heavy work.

They moved about the house after dark. Ellie hung over the cradle, and Laurie Jean stopped to watch, wanting to pat the girl's child-soft face but stopped by the woman's body that at thirteen bent protectively over the month-old baby. Opal rested within the rough wood shaped by her father, wrapped in the extravagance with which he had greeted the birth of his first living child, a pink wool blanket bound by satin ribbon.

While Ellie washed the supper dishes, Laurie ironed her husband's mining clothes, watching the wrinkles disappear into widening black stains. Free from pain now, weak and at peace, the woman—married at sixteen, eighteen now, her hands hard with work, a faint line of pain over her brows left there by extended labor and then after the birth a week of bleeding, her ears receptive to the murmur of crickets and frogs—felt night air touch her coolly, wisping over her hot face as it combated the iron, the too-large fire that was just dying down. She set the iron down and paused, regarding her baby's face. "Opal" from the frail, exotic heroine who emerged triumphant as a well-wed lady in an old novel that Laurie had taken from the school library. Opal's book had had a colored frontispiece in which the heroine, her head somewhat canted, faced the world with eyes resembling those of a crippled calf to whom Laurie Jean at ten had given her budding heart. A long fragile neck gently fell into a long frail body covered entirely in ruffled white and ribbonry. Laurie had envied the preternaturally long emaciated fingers wanly refusing to touch a vase of pink roses and blue forget-me-nots. "Elizabeth" was Andy's grandmother's name. As the old woman removed her corncob pipe from withered lips and pushed her balding head into the baby's face, and, sucking air past her toothless gums, cackled with delight, Laurie stiffened with a desire to pull the baby away. Her own grandmother was disappointed that "Opal" had not been "Laura," a name that had descended to the grandmother from a great-great-grandmother and had been given again to her youngest grandchild (conceived unexpectedly seven years after the youngest of Laurie's five living brothers) not out of pride but out of history. "Opal" struck her as an empty bit of foolishness, and with her eyes though not, ever, in words, she communicated this to her granddaughter, who looked away stubbornly, guiltily.

Still standing at the ironing board, Laurie lifted her sweating feet from the cooling floor, one after the other, and rubbed them against the back of her legs. Ellie hung up the drying towel and said, "Think I'll just go out and sit on the porch for a little while." The crickets sang, and the frogs chirped, and a whippoorwill came near to spend his shrill sad throat. Opal Elizabeth moved in her cradle. Andy was coming home from town with strawberry jam for tomorrow's morning's biscuits. The milk had turned, and she would wield the dasher until the butter sailed to the top and clung to the wooden pole and came out clotted to be put into the blue dish her mother had given her, pouring off the milk and beating until the butter swirled, a single cloud to be tasted with a fingertip and set into cold water to hold it for the biscuits and strawberry jam.

As she took the dasher from its nails on the wall, Ellie came back through the door, latching it behind her. "Some men are coming up the road, carryin' on. They sound pretty drunk to me."

Laurie laughed at her. "Maybe they're comin' courtin'," she teased. "Better go and comb your hair, Ellie May."

The girl blushed, pleased but still uncomfortable. "I don't like the way they're carryin' on."

Voices rose and fell, stilling the whippoorwill. The men drunkenly called for Andrew. They threatened him. Laurie felt the bulk of the hill pressing against the house. "Maybe we better turn off the light," she whispered, and the younger girl, reaching above the yellow-and-white checked oilcloth of the table, hit the switch, her child-soft face disappearing.

Feet stamped on the porch, and someone shouted

angrily, "Come on out of there, Johnson."

Ellie drew in her breath, and Laurie reached over to grab her arm. The drunken men must belong to that bunch Andrew and her brother used to run around with before they got married. She remembered the bitterly disapproving look on the taciturn face of her father, who worked in the mines and once a month preached at the Sarvis Creek Baptist Church. "Bootlegging," he said, laying down the law to her brother, "poker playing. And worse." His son had turned away sullenly and gone out the door, winking at Laurie Jean.

Scattered mutterings. Sound of guns being cocked.

"They's only me here," she yelled.

A bullet slammed through the door, and Opal began to cry loudly.

"Hand me that gun," Laurie said. Ellie gave her the trembling shotgun, unloaded, and she shoved its barrel out the front window. "Just you come on now, just you come on."

Silence perhaps, and perhaps somebody said, "Aw, he ain't in there. I got no quarrel with the woman." More muttering, and then off they went, the night closing behind them. She hushed me, rocking me, staring at the hole above the table, while Ellie sat mutely on the bed.

When I was quieted, she touched Ellie's arm and, when Ellie drew back, said, "Come on now," and, with me hidden inside the pink blanket tightly in her arms, they sneaked out the back door in case somebody was left behind to keep watch for Andrew, and went off down the road to warn him. They moved down that rocky road picking their barefooted way to "the hump" where they climbed up on the ridge beneath the stiff-feathered pine, their bodies chilling in the running spring night that slowed to a halt, waiting with them, until his footsteps sounded a benison. Having got out of an uncle's truck at the foot of the hollow, he came toward them, shoulders bent under his load, head bent in midnight thought. Laurie waited until he was below them and murmured his name. He threw down the sack of potatoes and turned like a young bear before recognition penetrated, and he relaxed. "What the Sam Hill are you two doing here," and seeing me, his child, "with Opal Elizabeth out in the night air?"

Sitting in the kitchen's cold light, holding the ancient cards, I watch my mother's image, eyes gray shadows, shoulders hunched over the baby in its pink blanket, pulling her body in to deny the threat it had received.

Opal rose and went to her parents' bedroom door and whispered, "Mommy," returning to the familiar diminutive that New York had changed to, "Mom." The older woman threw on a robe and followed her back to the kitchen. Opal began to cry. Laurie sat down at the kitchen table and hugged her. "When you were born," she whispered, "you know what your Mamaw said?"

Opal shook her head.

"'Maybe she'll go see the world like you always wanted to.'"

"Do you remember the night Daddy left you and his cousin alone and the drunks came? I was a baby."

"What are you talking about, Opal?"

"After they left, the two of you took me and went to meet Daddy."

Her mother frowned, thinking back. "Oh, *that*," she said. "Who told you about it?"

"Daddy told me."

"You know how your Daddy likes a good story."

Opal realized that this tale that had so struck her imagination was a minor incident in her mother's life. "I'm scared, Mom. That's why I didn't tell you. I thought you would be scared, too."

"What are you scared about?"

"What if the baby is born dead. What if Sam leaves me?"

"That going to happen?" her mother asked.

"We've been having fights."

"About the baby?"

"No. About little things. It's nothing, but people just pick up and go."

"Honey, people do that everywhere nowadays. Why ain't he with you now?"

"He's behind grading papers, and he had to teach a Saturday class."

"He might've found a way to come with you."

"I didn't want him to, to tell you the truth. I didn't want a stranger around when I saw Mamaw."

"He's not a stranger to you, Opal."

"I didn't want to have the baby," Opal cried. "Not yet."

"You still feel that way?"

"I wanted Mamaw to rock her. Now that won't happen. Mamaw will be gone before she arrives."

"Hush, Opal."

The two women clung to each other. In the morning, they would go to the hospital where Opal's grandmother lay in a stupor. "Will you come and stay with me when the baby's due?" Opal asked.

Laurie's fingers closed around her daughter's hand. "Well, I was afraid you wasn't going to ask."

"Let's name her now," Opal said and felt as though she might tear her daughter out of the darkness.

The Wedding Ring Quilt

M y mother was ill that year, and we did not go home to Kentucky at all. I was busy applying to colleges and hardly noticed it when Mamaw wrote that my cousin Shelley had gone to Ohio to stay with her father for a while. My mother shook her head. Then, just after I had been given the scholarship to Michigan State, we received a wedding invitation. Shelley was getting married to somebody in Columbus at a Methodist church, and the reception was going to be held at an unfamiliar address. "That's not your Uncle Jimmy's place," Mommy said. She wrote a letter to Mamaw, and not long before the wedding received a short, painfully grammatical letter from my grandmother: Shelley had met this man somewhere in Columbus, a lawyer with a lot of money. He wasn't from home. Nobody knew his family. Nobody knew anything about him. "The Lord only knows what I'll do without her," Mamaw wrote.

Reading the letter, I found myself uneasy. I thought of my frail grandmother and of the white frame house and the hills. In my grandmother's house, there was an old ironbound trunk that my great-grandmother had brought with her from New Jersey not long before the end of the nineteenth century. My grandmother kept her best quilts in that trunk, including a Wedding Ring quilt made of swatches of brocade dresses that had belonged to her own mother. Once a year, in the deep summer, my grandmother would unfold the Wedding Ring quilt and lay it across her bed for us to see: its gold and blue rings afloat on a white background. Mamaw had intended to pass it on to her own daughter, but then there were three of them, and she couldn't bear to single one out.

My great-grandmother had also brought with her a sum of money, a dowry, I suppose, and her husband bought with it a small but fertile valley farm. She must have soon put aside her finery and got down to the business of birthing and rearing a family, milking cows and feeding hogs, and taking care of the garden, while my great-grandfather hoed the cornfields and cut timber. He used his farm well, and when some Eastern speculators came around buying up mineral rights, he was one of the few landowners to withstand them.

By the time my grandmother was ten many of the great oak trees on the hillsides had been felled, and heavy erosion had ruined the neighbor's house and garden. By the time she was thirteen, a coal mine had been constructed at the opposite end of the long, narrow valley, and the neighbor and his three sons, one only twelve, went underground. The following year there was an explosion, and twenty were killed, including the neighbor and his youngest son. My great-grandfather hated the mine.

Soon after her sixteenth birthday, Mamaw ran away from home to marry the young miner who had been courting her after church meeting on Sundays. She went to live in the next county, in a log cabin on a thickly wooded hillside. Papaw's wages were small, and often supper was cornbread and a mess of wild greens. They would not accept the chickens and hog and even cow that her parents, relenting, pressed them to take. Mamaw became a poor woman with a huge brood of children. They picked mayapple and ginseng to eke out their income.

When her father died, he divided up the farm among his sons, leaving for his only daughter the house and three surrounding acres. Papaw and Mamaw and their children moved in with my grieving great-grandmother. The sturdy white two-story house was surrounded by fruit trees and, beyond, by waving broomsage, and, beyond that, by those green, green hills—poplars, elms, birches, and oaks, and black walnuts and hickories, and spicewood and sassafras and sumac, a litany I used to know—and in spring by the lush rose tips on the bare-limbed redbuds and then amid the mist and newly green the white blossoms of sarvis trees.

Shelley was born there in 1938, at the hands of my grandmother, who had added to her talents for survival the art of midwifery. Shelley's mother died two days later, and within the month her father left for Ohio to find work. Shelley remained behind with Mamaw.

When I was born, my family still lived in the valley. Daddy was loading coal in a ramshackle nonunion mine. Mommy tended the garden, kept the three-room shack clean, tended us. On weekends we spent most of our time at Mamaw's. Uncles and aunts and cousins would come, too. Sometimes when I am unhappy, I close my eyes and am again in my grandmother's house. I remember each room, the quilts on the featherbeds, the blue and white wallpaper in the living room, the coal stove where she made gravy and chicken and dumplings and berry cobblers. The path to the large old garden with the cherry tree in the center. And the path across the field and up the hill to the coal bank in whose cool dark watery depths we placed the milk and butter to keep cool. And at night, flames of the kerosene lamps flickering in the shadowed rooms.

My mother says that in my baby years, Shelley treated me as though I was a big doll baby. What I remember is tagging along behind her and her best friend when school let out: the one-room schoolhouse on Sarvis Mountain. From the recitation bench up front, I would turn around to make sure that Shelley was watching out for me as I traversed the long distance from the bench to the blackboard to do my sums. At lunch, she would take my drinking cup from its hook on the wall and fill it for me from the bucket of water that came from the well of the family who lived across the dirt road.

Shelley and her friend April had secrets, all of which seemed to be about boys. At noon hours there was always a boy talking to Shelley at the back of the schoolhouse. Shelley had long brown hair and large blue eyes. I wanted to look just like her.

During the war years, Daddy got a job at a small coal mine, but he learned that he could earn much more in the Columbus factory where Shelley's father worked. The uncles came and helped us load our belongings into the back of the old pickup truck. My brother and sister and I sat in the truck bed, peering back through the opening in the tarpaulin. Mamaw and Shelley pressed their faces close to the hole, and then they were gone. The house, the creek, the valley, the hills lurched by and disappeared.

In Ohio, some kids called us hillbillies. Mommy cried, and Daddy came home from work with stooped shoulders and blank eyes. Once every month or two, we'd pile into the pickup and go home to Mamaw's house. Each time we went, it seemed another uncle or aunt or cousin had left, looking for work, but Mamaw and Shelley were there, and the house, the garden, the hills. I swore to myself that someday I would come back home.

Shelley was in the eighth grade when Mamaw told Mommy that some man from over on Apple Creek had come courting. Mamaw had sent him away.

In the following year, Daddy got a job in a Ford plant in the Detroit area. It was a good-paying job, and we moved to a quiet area outside the city where our Uncle Silas, Daddy's older brother, already lived. Mommy had a second cousin on the next street. The school was rough but not too bad. Traitor and mutineer, I had worked hard at losing my hillbilly sound. My father laughed at what he called the beans-and-buttermilk noises I now made. Eventually, I had friends, and so did Cecil and Lucille. My English teacher discovered my passion for reading and talked to me of going to college. Home was too far away now to think of going there more than once or twice a year.

Suddenly I was an introverted junior. My current English teacher was telling the principal to get me a scholarship. When I told my parents, their eyes shone proudly while their arms went desperately around me. Cecil was working at the Ford plant with Daddy and was engaged to a Michigan girl. Lucille was a bank teller, living at home but spending her time with friends. She was saving up money to move into an apartment. They no longer went home to Kentucky with us. But I still looked forward to those trips south as though they were pilgrimages.

Mamaw and Shelley always treated us as though we had never left. We never talked in that house about the illusory Michigan that filled our everyday lives but picked up the thread where it had been broken. Cousin Sue Anne had just had her third baby, a boy, born in the hospital (Mamaw had midwifed the first two). Uncle Jesse had black lung (Uncle Jesse was there that evening, sitting by the fireplace breathing noisily). Cora Harbin got herself a job in the hardware store in town. Billy Orson's two boys got hurt in a slate fall at the mine. Piney Crawford had cancer of the stomach. And Delia Ann and the younguns were coming over after meeting tomorrow. Mamaw and Shelley had just picked a peck of wild strawberries and got scared by a rattlesnake. Shelley killed it with a hoe.

Shelley talked and laughed with my parents but was now shy and abrupt with me. She had finished high school and was working as a secretary in the mining office. Mamaw said that three men so far had asked her to marry. "I guess Shelley kin afford to pick 'n'choose," she said. "When I go, the house is hers."

I looked enviously around at the now shabby house, through the windows at the flowering yard, and, farther off, the green hills with yet some morning mist floating in the hollers.

Mommy was feeling better, and Daddy had some vacation time. They decided to go to Shelley's wedding. Mamaw had written that Uncle Franklin and Uncle Clarence and Aunt Delia and their spouses were going to be there, and she was riding up with Uncle Jesse.

We got lost not far north of Columbus and arrived at the church just in time. It was a red brick edifice with stained-glass windows and a large white portal. In the paved parking lot were long, shiny cars. We had last gone to church in my eighth year, in the single room that the Rag'lar Baptists had built on the far side of Sarvis Mountain.

Inside the edifice, an organ was playing. On the right side of the aisle were men in suits and women wearing lipstick and earrings that flickered in their short, curly hair. An usher in a tuxedo hurried us down the aisle to join a dark little woman with a wrinkled face and a cheap, travel-wrinkled dress. Mamaw's hair was drawn back in its usual bun. She peered up at us and said, "Hit shore is good to see you-all. I was scairt you'd git lost." The uncles nodded at us uneasily, their red faces shining above hard starched collars. When they smiled, I saw the gaps where teeth were missing. My aunts—faces unadorned, floral dresses badly cut—smiled, too.

"We thought you was never gonna git here, honey," Aunt Delia whispered to me. I looked away.

The groom was a man of about thirty. He looked a little somber, but splendidly so, I thought, with his compact, smart-suited frame and wavy haircut and the shaft of knowing light that fell from behind his dark eyelashes. He and the best man and the families on the right side of the aisle seemed to me to belong to some world where refrigerators were so full that one used their contents only sparingly, a world where sickness and death, suffering and loss hardly seemed to exist. Shelley was coming down the aisle, dressed in a long ivory dress, her lovely hair piled high and her blue eyes alight. One hardly noticed the awkward old man with the crippled arm (he had been hurt in a factory accident) who piloted her.

The reception was held at the home of the groom's parents. ("I never heard of sich a thang," Mamaw said.) His parents came forward to introduce themselves. The father had a country twang, but his wife spoke distantly, tugging the sleeve of her silk jacket as though she were on familiar terms with it. They soon moved away, down the aisle. Those of us who belonged to Shelley stood in a dense, little clump after the aunts had made one or two half-hearted forays into an unreceptive crowd. No one took champagne but Daddy, who was generally understood to be something of a rebel. After a while, Shelley came over and hugged Mamaw. Mamaw clung to her. "I give her the Wedding Ring," she said. "Like I promised." I felt sharply jealous. Shelley looked over at her husband, and he beckoned to her, and she left to join the laughing groom in a crowd of laughing people.

That August, a letter written in Shelley's careful, schoolgirl's hand came for me. She asked me to come down and spend a weekend. My mother and father looked at each other.

"How long they bin married now?" Daddy asked.

"Since March. And they got back from Hawaii in April. They still ain't gone down home."

"Aaaiih," my father said. "Let her go. I reckon it'll be all right."

Two weeks later, I took a Greyhound to Columbus. It was the first time I had taken a long trip by myself. Smoothing the neat little dress Mommy had chosen, I watched the road approach and disappear. When we neared Columbus, I went into the smelly restroom at the back of the bus and applied forbidden red lipstick.

Shelley met me at the station; as she walked toward me I saw that she was limping. She was wearing a slim, narrow skirt, a filmy white blouse, and pumps with three-inch heels. I thought the shoes must be causing the limp. "Lord, honey, hit's—it's good to see you," she said.

"How was Hawaii?"

"It was *beautiful*. I never seen the sea before. We went swimmin' ever day. And Ed took me to see the volcano." She fished a bunch of keys from her purse and announced shyly, "I'm driving us home. Ed bought me a car."

"We're going down to see Mamaw next week," I told her as we moved through city streets in a small glossy car.

"Ed says we cain't go this summer. He's too busy. I got a letter from her yesterday. She says the corn is full of punkins this year. Cora Harbin quit her job at the hardware store. Got mad at him for bossin' her around and up and quit."

She pulled in beside a stone ranch house sitting on about an acre of grassy land. The big yard was filled with fine old elms. Another, larger car sat in the open garage. Shelley's husband met us at the front door and smiled, and kissed me on the cheek. He took my suitcase and steered me to a small white bedroom. The bedspread was a white satiny material, and on the dark wood of the bureau were red flowers sitting in a crystal vase. Shelley came into the room and said, "You like it?"

"What a question, Shelley," he said. I saw him shake his head minutely at her.

"But I do like it," I insisted, looking at them, at how pleasing they looked.

"Edward bought the flowers this morning," Shelley said. "His ma give us the bedspread."

We returned to the living room, which had a long, white,

49

nubby couch flanked by dark shiny tables. In a corner stood a huge urn filled with glossy leaves. On the wall above the couch hung a large painting of water lilies. "Ed bought the furniture," Shelley said. "His ma gave us the painting." "Just a Monet reproduction," Edward said. "But a good one."

"It was courageous of you to take a bus," he added. "Shelley, dear, bring us some iced tea."

She returned bearing a silver tray with tall glasses of tea. "I don't put sugar in it," she warned. "Ed don't like sugar in his tea."

"*Doesn't*, darling," he said. "*Doesn't* like sugar in his tea."

"Doesn't like sugar in his tea." She giggled nervously.

He pulled her down beside him on the nubby couch. I looked at his wavy hair and his gray suit and his even white teeth and was half in love with him myself.

Shelley made roast chicken and a salad for dinner. Edward served us white wine in stemmed glasses. A half glass of it made me tipsy. I had read somewhere that people with good manners ate singlehandedly, so I kept my left hand in my lap. Edward talked about news items, about Hawaii, and asked me about my plans for college. Shelley was mostly silent, continually making quick smiles that unfolded briefly in his direction and then collapsed.

After dinner, Edward went back downtown to his office, and Shelley and I looked at the photographs he had taken in Hawaii. "Let's go downtown tomorrow," she said, hugging me. "We kin go shoppin'."

"Oh, yes," I said, but I was no longer sure. I looked at the photograph of the two of them taken on the beach by a passing stranger and thought that when I went to college, perhaps I would meet a man like Edward, but now I asked myself if I wanted to.

So the next day, Shelley and I went downtown. Her limp seemed less pronounced, and I asked, "Did you twist your foot?" "No," she said, stopping and looking at me for a long moment, "I didn't twist it." She seemed about to add something but turned instead and went through the revolving door into Lazarus's department store. We rode the escalator up to Junior Dresses, and Shelley asked my permission to buy me a dress. "I got plenty of money," she said, opening her purse. I let her talk me into it, although I knew what my father would say. Excitedly I tried on the new fall dresses and finally chose a red one with a big skirt.

When we got back to the stone house, we pulled off our shoes and dropped our purchases. Shelley lay down on the white couch in the cool, dim living room while I sat in a plump armchair.

"Do you have the Wedding Ring quilt on your bed?" I asked, wanting to see it.

"I put it away for safekeeping," she said. She went to a hall closet and returned with a large plastic bag from which she tenderly removed the quilt, the shining gold and blue brocade aswim in the dark room. We talked about Mamaw's blackberry jam and Uncle Jesse's black lung and Cora Harbin's lack of employment. Then she put away the quilt, and we waited for Edward.

I went to church with them the next morning, the church where they had been married. Edward's father came over and hugged Shelley and then went hurrying back to his wife, who was talking to another woman and did not look up. Shelley drove me to the bus station. As I looked out the dingy window at her upturned face, I felt some secret complicity between us, some outlaw knowledge.

That fall, I went off to my freshman year at Michigan State. (I wore the red dress on the first day of classes.) At first, I spent most of my time working on getting high grades and winning the approval of my professors and I kept to my room on weekends. Little by little, two girls on my dorm corridor proved too friendly and forthcoming for my defenses, and there was also a tall pleasant boy who spoke to me sometimes. My new friends treated college as though it were some necessary disease to which the middle class was prone. Soon I began to cultivate an ironical air, sure all the while that a charmed world, a world I now sought, lay out of sight beyond the curved driveways of the bourgeoisie.

There was a bad snow that Christmas, so we did not drive to Kentucky, though Mommy was worried about her own mother. She said she hadn't heard from Mamaw for several weeks. "What about Shelley?" I asked, twirling around the room in my red dress. Mommy turned her face away. "I *guess* she's all right," she said. I only half noticed her reservation, having in mind other things, Christmas and my brother's forthcoming wedding and my sister's new apartment, my life at college, and the tall, pleasant boy.

When spring break came, we did go down to see Mamaw. I felt that old excitement as we crossed the broad, broad Ohio and caught our first glimpse of the hills. It was lovely weather that day, sunny, both chilled and warm, the sky watercolor blue decorated by wind-tossed clouds. The first green was showing in the woods. The redbud trees were rosy-winged.

As we rode along the ever-narrowing road deeper into the hills, as we drove finally into Mamaw's valley, I saw as though for the first time the shacks on the hillsides, the poorly dressed people sitting on their porches. And there, at last, was Mamaw's house, the paint peeled now, the porch swing replaced long ago by a rusty-edged white and green glider.

Sitting in the glider were two women. As we pulled up into the yard, I saw that Shelley was with Mamaw. Shelley had a huge blue bruise on the left side of her face. Mamaw ran into the yard to meet us, but my cousin sat still.

"What happened to her?" Mommy whispered.

"That no-good husband of hers, that's what happened," Mamaw said.

Mommy went onto the porch and hugged Shelley. Like a child who sees a grown-up in trouble, I stood in the yard dumbfounded and embarrassed. Supported by my mother's arm, Shelley came into the yard and greeted me as though I were a sister. "I hear you're doin' real well at college," she said.

"Shelley's been goin' to school too," Mamaw said. "He didn't want her talking like no hillbilly."

"I took an evening English class," Shelley said.

"Well, you're well shut of him," Daddy burst out, and Mommy and Mamaw nodded their heads, but Shelley said nothing.

On Sunday, Shelley and I made our old trip up to the coal bank. Shelley admired my new haircut. "Edward bought me this dress," she said shyly. "Isn't it pretty?"

I didn't know what to say. I had been kissed a couple of times by the tall pleasant boy, and that was the extent of my experience, but even in that, I had felt the deep tide.

When we left the next day, Mamaw and Shelley were standing on the porch. Shelley was dressed in an old cotton dress. She looked again as though she belonged there, in Mamaw's house. Mamaw had her hand on Shelley's arm.

A month later, Mommy told me on the phone that Shelley had gone back to her husband.

Summer arrived. I came home and got a job at McDonald's. Daddy and Mommy went to Kentucky for a week and returned shaking their heads. "Your Mamaw's gittin' old," Mommy said to me. "She ain't heard nothin' from Shelley since she went back."

I took a week's vacation in late summer and visited a friend in New York. The bus entered the city at night, a dark new continent with clustering towers of light. My friend and I went to see a play, to the ballet, to a foreign movie. We walked through streets thick with varied people and variegated goods. Surely I had entered the charmed world.

Reluctantly I came home and went back to school. Two years passed, during which I became more and more involved in the life of my friends. Impatiently I would go home for short vacations, tearing myself away from the tall pleasant boy, with whom I now indulged in heavy petting. We talked of getting engaged, and he wanted me to go with him to Pittsburgh the next time he visited his parents. I told my parents about the invitation. Anxiously they asked again what kind of boy he was, how did he behave toward me. Anxiously my mother told me not to let him go too far. I laughed at their worries, resenting their unhappy insistence, their claim upon my new life.

So there was a sad distance in my mother's voice the day she called to tell me that Shelley had killed herself. Shocked out of my self-absorption, I felt our grief and its more general burden. We cried together. "We're going down for the funeral tomorrow," she said hesitantly.

"Oh, I'm coming, too. But where is she being buried? Columbus?"

"No," my mother said urgently. "She was done separated from that man. She's goin' home."

I did not get to Detroit until three in the morning, and at five, we left for Kentucky. As we sped through the lonesome dark, Mommy told me that Shelley had driven out of town, found a river, and jumped in. She had been showing up at Uncle James's apartment frequently in the past year. "Well, I just can't take it any longer," she would say to her father.

"Jimmy would ask her why," Mommy said, "and she'd say that man didn't think she was good enough for him. 'I try to be like he wants. Lord knows I try.' The last time she came, she said that was it, he was seeing another woman. 'One of his own kind. Give me some money, Daddy, for a bus ticket. I want to go home.' But the next day, while your uncle was at work, she drove to the river."

It was a home funeral. Shelley's body lay in an open casket in Mamaw's front room. She was dressed in the long pink dress Mamaw had made for her graduation, and her hair was pinned on top of her head.

Funerals last for days down home. My cousin Leroy, Uncle Clarence's oldest son, was one of the preachers. He said that God had wanted Shelley to stay home with her own kind. I felt a superstitious dread.

The uncles carried the casket up the hill to the graveyard where my great-grandmother's stillborn babies lay and my great-grandmother and my great-grandfather and Papaw and Shelley's mother and Uncle Jesse and several more. Plain stone markers stood at the head of the grassy mounds beneath trees that belonged to the old forest. I looked across the valley to another line of hills, smoky in the distance, and then down at the living green, at tree branches afloat in a small wind, and I felt a strange, deep familiarity, an intimate self that would always slumber elsewhere and only awaken in the hills.

Afterward, as we sat on Mamaw's porch watching the lightning bugs, Mamaw cried out, "I want the Wedding Ring quilt back."

My parents and the uncles and aunts nodded their heads.

Aunt Delia said, "We shore don't want that devil to keep it."

Leroy muttered, "They shore ain't goin' to send it back."

"Then somebody better go git it," Uncle Clarence said. They all nodded their heads again.

Mamaw looked at me. "I reckon Nettie might could git it." They nodded their heads once more. My parents looked anxious. "It might not be safe," my father said.

"Oh, Daddy," I admonished him. "What's he going to do to me in broad daylight." My superior knowledge of the bourgeoisie, gained from those mysterious years at college, won the day.

A few weeks later, I called the number Shelley had given me. I called for several days in a row, but no one answered. "Call his parents," my sympathetic roommate said. I got the number from directory assistance and dialed. Edward's mother answered and said that he was out of town. I told her why I was calling. "I'm sure he doesn't want it," she said frigidly. "Come and get it, if you wish." We fixed a time and date, and two days later I once again took a Greyhound bus to Columbus. This time there was no one to meet me at the station. I took a city bus. Feeling unexpectedly young and vulnerable, I rang the bell. Edward's father opened the door. His shoulders were stooped, and he seemed a full two inches shorter than I remembered. His face was heavy and old and sad as he looked at me. "I remember you," he said.

"I've been waiting." He reached out and took my hand and held on to it, "My son didn't treat her right," he said. "That's the sorrow *we* have to bear."

He went inside and returned with the quilt in its heavy plastic bag. Then he insisted on driving me to the hotel where I would spend the night. We rode silently. I got out of the car and could think of nothing more to say than "Thank you."

Carefully I carried the Wedding Ring quilt, still in its plastic bag, to my room. I spread the quilt out on the bed and thought that I would return it now to Mamaw's house. She would put it in the ironbound trunk, and perhaps someday the Wedding Ring would go to a bride who would keep it in the hills. I cried for my cousin and for myself, who had begun to realize that there are no charmed worlds except those that we create, piece by piece, from our histories.

Cresco

When the young woman heard her cousin say the word "Cresco," she felt a dark thrill, the kind a religious pessimist might feel on hearing "Armageddon." Her repulsion was all the greater because her cousin belonged to the world before Cresco, the childhood paradise that she carried about with her like a magnificent jewel. Her husband, who had just come up beside her, said, "Cresco, where's that?" and she left her cousin to enlighten him while she herself slipped away to another corner of the yellow-and-white striped tent.

It was a lovely day in southern Ohio, a light-filled summer day with a few steep white clouds marking the blue depths of the sky. The week before there had been plenty of rain, and the trees were a clean, clear green, the yard flowers intransigently vivid. Children in bright clothes played here and there like noisy butterflies. Through the tent opening, Anita could also see her plump grandmother sitting restfully in a green chair, her aging children, including Anita's mother, bending solicitously about.

The occasion for the tent and the barbecued chicken on the grill and the catered salads on the picnic table and the desserts inside on the kitchen table was her grandmother's seventieth birthday. Grandma Hallitt now lived in Ohio with her widowed daughter Victoria, and Anita's mother, who had moved nearby, was throwing the party. Many people had come up from Osier County, the home county in Kentucky.

Anita herself had flown in from Philadelphia with her husband. They argued on the plane. He had been working long hours and asked why, if they must leave home, they had not spent the time at his parents' vacation cottage in the Poconos. They had been fighting a lot lately. He pointed out that Anita had visited her mother last month and then spent one weekend showing Philadelphia to her brother Bobby and his family. She pointed out in turn that his own family lived outside Philadelphia and claimed their attention at least one evening a week, if not a whole day and evening.

"They don't require *all* our attention, though," he answered.

"Neither does mine."

"They don't have to. You give it to them anyway."

She sat there remembering Osier County, counting its green hills and silver hollows like beads on a rosary.

Weekdays Anita spent alone in their roomy ranch house, except for Maria, who came twice a week to clean. A landscape service mowed the lawn and tended the flowers. Occasionally her next-door neighbor came by—the one who didn't have any children—or Anita crossed the lawn and reciprocated. Less frequently, Anita and Stuart were invited to dinner or a party, or they themselves entertained. These were Stuart's friends. Some of them had attended grade school with him. Anita herself had developed no close bonds in Philadelphia. She spent time on the phone with old college friends.

She had taught school in Ohio while Stuart was finishing his MBA and then in a suburb of Philadelphia for the first two years of their marriage. She was often bored. When he received an unexpected promotion, and their income rose exponentially, she gladly quit teaching, thinking that after a few months of leisure, she would go back to school and get a Ph.D. in English. The few months had stretched into two more years. When she allowed herself to think about it, she felt vaguely lost. She was not attached to the house or the neighborhood or even, she thought more and more often, to her husband. She did unnecessary housework, started ambitious reading programs and dropped them. Now Stuart wanted to have a baby.

Standing in the tent opening, Anita spotted a sister here, a brother there until her eyesight encompassed all six of them. As children, they had traveled together from state to state as their father looked for a satisfactory place, a place where he would find work but which would feel like Osier County, where there was no work. All of them had managed to make it to the birthday party, even the brother who lived in California with his Japanese wife. Funds from their dead father's black-lung settlement were paying for the party, as they had paid for the house and the large, tree-strewn yard.

Anita's cousin Oma had said, "We were over to Cresco the other day visiting Aunt Ruth," and she went on to talk about how the mine was doing nowadays, about Aunt Ruth and Cousin Jason and Cousin Suzette. Anita looked back into the tent and saw that Stuart was still talking to Oma. There really wasn't much to know about Cresco, she thought, beyond the dirt and aggravation of the place. Her family had been unhappy there.

Anita never mentioned Cresco to her husband. She had told him very little about the negative things in her life. When they were dating, she had plucked her early childhood from its velvet case and displayed it. It was as much her fault as his that he had viewed her early life as a kind of glamorous folk-tale. He himself belonged to the great American middle class, a suburban child who had done well in school and played soccer and gotten an MBA at a decent college, where they had met. She had been on a scholarship. She felt that she was his one weakness. Would he define her life in Cresco as a kind of sociological tract? He laughed now at something her cousin had said, and she experienced minor jealousy. Oma and Anita had not seen each other for about a decade, which was how long it had been since Anita had visited Kentucky with her parents, the summer after her senior year in college. The family always went to Kentucky in the summer, and Anita's memories of Osier County were green and silver.

Her memories of Cresco were quite another matter.

They had come there freshly from Osier County on a sunny fall day after Ruth's Gerald got his brother-in-law a job in the Cresco mine. After the gentle hills of their home place, they were spooked by the grand russet mountains with vertical roads that seemed to fold back on themselves.

The house was gray in a row of gray houses with tiny, bald yards. In front of the houses in successive waves were the muddy dirt road, the railroad tracks where cars of coal went by, and a mountainous slag heap. In back, the yard dipped over a steep, garbage-slicked bank to the gray river. She still remembered the frozen faces of her parents as they avoided each other's eyes that first day. Her mother had been pregnant with Carlene.

The house itself was sound enough, and the younger children were much taken with the idea of having an upstairs. It was more spacious than their small white house (between two green hills) in Osier County had been, and Anita had to share only with her sister Jeannette. When she asked, her father brought home some weathered planks, and she borrowed tools from his toolbox to construct a bookcase. Bobby had finished it for her.

In the mornings, they had to be quiet so their father, who worked the night shift, could get some sleep. They were not allowed to play beyond the dreary yard, although there was a meadow nearby, its wildflowers half-wilted with coal breezes.

There was no running water in the house and no well to draw water from. A spigot sat atop a rusty pipe that spiked the north corner of the yard, on the opposite side from the outhouse. "Tainted water," their father called it. "It'll do for washing ourselves and our clothes." They got their drinking and cooking water from a spring on the other side of the river, a job given to Anita and Bobby. She remembered them that first day setting out across the swinging bridge that stretched above the river, sagging a little in the middle, its rusty wire topes swaying in the wind.

There was a line of red-leaved maples on the other side. As you neared the bridge's end, you could see beyond the trees a small green valley where several white-framed houses sat. Rows of corn in various stages of growth scratched the sky. At the bottom of a large mound had sat a broad, clear-watered spring with a dipping bucket roped to a post. Up above, on the mound, was an old farmhouse where an old man often sat on the porch. Their father would wave at him, but he never waved back.

Their school had sat in a graveled yard. There was an old, wooden merry-go-round and an iron Maypole. Children who fell from the Maypole lost skin to the gravel. There were rowdy children whose favorite word seemed to be "Fuck." Many of the girls wore lipstick and earrings. Meg Henders invited Anita to come visit her one Saturday and after Anita begged and begged, her father dropped her off on his way to buy a truck part in town. When he came back, she was wearing a pair of dangling earrings and Meg's red lipstick. He never let her go again.

Vince, her youngest brother, who had been very talkative, grew quiet, and one day he disappeared for several hours. Frantically, their mother sent Anita to the grocery to call the mine and ask that her husband come home. The man behind the counter wouldn't let Anita use the phone, but a miner in the store overheard her and said he'd go to the mine himself and bring her father home. When they came, several other miners were with them, and they fanned out, the lights on their hard mining hats like giant lightning bugs in the twilight. Late in the night, Anita found Vince asleep behind the washing machine. He had not been there when they looked earlier on. He never told anyone where he had been.

"Whip this boy," their crying mother said to her husband, hugging Vince to her.

"I don't have the heart."

A busty woman with a heavily powdered face taught the eighth grade. She read Gothic novels to them the last hour of the day. Anita's mother shook her head at the content, as divulged to her by Anita.

One day Anita discovered blood on her panties. She didn't tell anyone but went to the rag box when she got home and folded up rags to put there. Her stomach hurt, low down. Maybe it was something called a period, but maybe she had malaria. When wash day came, her mother discovered blood on Anita's skirt. "It's something that happens to every girl," she said briefly behind a shut door. She gave her daughter some torn-up old sheets. They washed and bleached the bloody rags each month.

Around this time, Anita had surreptitiously borrowed one of her father's Zane Grey paperbacks and on reading a scene between a man and a woman, discovered in herself strong sensations that demanded relief.

"Don't touch yourself down there," Mommy said. "If you do, you'll hurt yourself."

On the last day of school, Anita wore a transparent blue nylon dress with white flocking on it that her mother had ordered for her from Montgomery Ward, along with a blue taffeta slip. Joanie, who lived next door, said, "I didn't know you could look like that. Want me to get you a date with my big brother?" Standing there in the muddy road, Anita felt threatened.

Then school was out, and for a blessed week they would go home to stay with Grandma Hallitt, still in Osierville. The apple trees were in bloom. Oma, who had been Anita's best friend, was in love with a boy who played basketball on the varsity team.

One September, Anita's father woke her up during the night. "Your mother's sick. I've got to take her to the hospital. You'll have to look after the kids." In Osier County, when their mom went to the hospital, Grandma Hallitt had come to stay. By the time Anita got downstairs, the car was pulling away from the yard. She could see her mother's face in profile, obscure in the moonlight. Anita thought probably they'd bring a baby home the next day, but she wasn't sure. She lay down in her parents' bed, waiting for daylight and the sound of feet coming down the stairs. She thought about the fact that she was lying on her father's side of the bed and wondered if that could cause her to have a baby.

Eventually her mother did come home with Carlene, but for several days Anita had tended the kids and cooked three meals a day and fixed her father's lunch bucket. He was rarely there, either at work or at the hospital. The kids didn't like minding her, and she had to shout at them. On the second day, Daddy said, "Your mother's lost a lot of blood. I thought we were going to lose her."

By July things seemed back to normal. "You've done enough, honey," Mommy said, stroking the hair back from Anita's face. They did not have a TV, and Anita grew tired of the country music on the radio. She took ten or twelve books at a time from the library and lost herself in them, inwardly vowing one day that she would go back to Osier County, the next that she would go to strange and faraway places.

On a hot August day, she picked up two empty buckets and headed across the swaying bridge, dreading it because a group of boys about her age were spending their summer sitting in the middle of the bridge, their legs dangling over the side. One of them, a wiry boy from whose house angry adult voices were often heard, would taunt her with obscenities as she went by. This time he let her pass by in silence. No one else was at the spring, so she sat a few minutes on a rock, watching a water spider, a small blue flower, a Monarch butterfly. When she returned, the boy stretched out a hand and grasped her thigh, laughing. She felt an anger that was almost levitating. Dropping one bucket, she poured the contents of the other one over his head. He called her names while the other boys laughed at him. When, crying, she made her way home with the empty buckets, her mother said, "Now, hush. You did the right thing."

Late afternoon shadows were stretching across Anita's mother's yard, defining the far corner on the other side of the lilac bushes to which Anita had wandered, divorcing herself from the crowd. It seemed distinctly sad to her now that she had avoided the thought of the boy on the bridge so much for so long. The deluge she had visited on him had been a handy substitute for a thrown rock or a devastating left hook. In a sudden access of fellowship, she pictured his wiry body many years later and hoped that he had at last escaped his angry house. Who knew? Maybe he was now Cresco's leading citizen or, perhaps, like her, he had vowed to get away. He had had unusual eyes, almond-shaped and green. What if he had gone away to college, too, to the same school that she had attended, and only chance forfended that, one August afternoon, she had rounded a corner and looked into his green eyes.

Anita's family had not remained in Cresco long beyond that summer. One day in early winter, her father had said, "I got a better job, over in Mingo County." Anita had asked her mother if she could go instead to live with Grandma Hallitt. "This time will be better," her mother said anxiously, holding the baby close. "We're going to live in what they call a prefab house, with running water. You'll be going to high school in town, and your daddy says he hears it's a good school." But Anita had carried with her the memory of Cresco. Over the years, she had managed to relegate the place to a far corner, but its residue in her consciousness was a dark knowledge that colored her perceptions. Although she was given to nostalgia and sometimes made special visits to gather up the different pieces of her life, she had never wanted to return to Cresco.

Her sister Jeannette's voice came from behind. "Anita, what are you doing off here by yourself? Everybody's leaving."

They returned to the other side of the lilac bushes to say goodbye to various aunts and uncles and cousins and children. After helping put the food away and washing dishes, Vince and Carlene took their spouses to motels. Bobby and Jeannette and Lorrain and their families got ready to leave for their homes close by. They would all return for an early dinner tomorrow. Anita hugged Grandma Hallitt, who said, "Come over and visit me and Victoria before you go back, you and that good-lookin' husband of yours."

He was standing by Bobby's pickup, deep in conversation with Bobby and Oma's husband, David. Probably talking about fishing. Bobby took fishing vacations, and angling was the one sport in which her husband indulged now. He was passionate about it. She liked that about him.

Oma, who was sitting by the newly cleared picnic table, said, "Come on over here and visit with me, Anita. I haven't had a chance to say two words to you."

"Does Suzette still live at Aunt Ruth's?" Anita asked, sitting down beside her cousin.

Oma's forehead creased, "No, honey, she don't. She

come back to Osierville, and she's working in a beauty salon. She gets the awfullest headaches. No health insurance."

"How are your kids?"

"Sylvie and Offie are doin' fine. Sylvie's got a little cold, though. I hated to leave her, but Mommy'll take good care of her. And we'll be back before dark."

"Remember that time we slipped up behind David and the Kotlow boy and you blew that whistle?"

Oma laughed. "Scared the livin' daylights out of them. Served 'em right for puttin' salt in our lemonade at the church dinner. But you don't want to know what happened to the Kotlows."

"What?"

"Some feller on drugs broke in and shot them dead, Ed and Sally Jean both, with a semiautomatic. Their kids are living with their grandma. And she's not doin' too well herself."

"It never was paradise, was it, Oma?"

Oma understood right away. "Well, honey, we were children. It's still God's green acre to me, though."

And they talked of this and that as only old friends can do. Oma went away with David then, promising to get up to Philadelphia sometime.

Lightning bugs were beginning to float around the yard like nether stars.

Anita and Stuart were left alone with Anita's mother. The older woman went indoors, leaving them on the front porch. "Did you enjoy yourself?" Anita asked politely.

"I'm tired," he said sullenly. "Is Jeannette going to have another baby?"

"She's four months gone," Anita said, forcing her voice to cheery heartiness. She had told him that she might agree to have a baby next year. She felt as though she were perched in a life that might not be the right one for her. Having a child was irrevocable.

He was standing over her and saying something urgently. "What?" she asked, staring into his angry eyes.

"I want to go back to Philly tonight."

"We'll have the baby," she said by way of answering, offering him a reluctant gift, knowing she was wrong to do it.

"You don't want to," he said with an edge of despair in his voice.

"Are you still angry?" she whispered.

"I don't know. I need some time alone."

She asked warily, "Will you be there when I get back?"

He looked warily back. "Yes, I'll be there. I'll pick you up at the airport next Saturday." He called a cab to take him to the airport in town. It would probably cost him sixty or seventy, she thought.

Anita wondered what they would say to each other when she got back. Looking through the screen door at the warm yellow light within, she let herself realize that she had called no place home since Osier County. No, she wouldn't have a child yet. She thought she would go back to school first, as she had originally planned. Maybe Stuart would still be there, maybe not. She hoped he would. Peering in at the dear form of her mother, Anita knew that she had to let go of her family long enough to make a home in the universe. It would not be in Osier County, but, if she were lucky, it would be lit by the memory of its green and silver light.

Paradise

The first time Fanny saw the city at night, she was lifted out of herself entirely by its eight million lights, or so she counted them, one for every inhabitant, its luminous structures hanging in the air like fairy-tale palaces. The intoxicating hugeness of it hovering in nature's milder night.

Later, of course, Fanny came to know its dreary, claustrophobic, criminal aspects, so much more real to the homeless hidden under bridges, drug addicts in dark alleys, and even to rebelling bourgeois and to older bourgeois who had their own brand of hell.

Fanny was not a bourgeois, though no one could ever have wanted more than she to be one, not from that moment when, going to visit her brother in an Ohio hospital, the rattling, dirty family car passed lovely estates and sham Tudor houses on the outskirts of Cincinnati. Here was paradise. Unlike the biblical paradise hedged about with thorns and floating on the very edge of Hell, into which one might fall if one so much as put a foot wrong while following Jesus's footsteps through the pearly gates. That other paradise she had known in Kentucky had, ironically enough, been snatched away by the bourgeois (she hadn't entirely conceptualized this fact at the time of that Ohio trip) when her father was laid off from his electrician's job at a mine owned by people in New York and Pittsburgh. Fanny had been a carefully shielded child in the little sage-green house on Sarvis Creek, nestled among apple and cherry trees, its domestic events accompanied by aeolian music and by the deeper sounds of the little creek that ran into the Osier River. All those definite articles had been hedges against the dangers of her father's life in the mines and her mother's life as a fragile woman bearing many children with the help of a midwife. Just as the love of a precariously comfortable extended family had walled out from the children the fear of too much poverty that besieged its adults.

In West Virginia, where her father found another mining job, they had lived in a coal camp, in a dirty-looking house with a slag heap in front. The tall West Virginia mountains, so much steeper than those that surrounded the little green house in Kentucky, cast the coal camp valley in deep shadow long before day was done and presented hairpin curves on which the dusty family car seemed to hang precariously. If one had money and a clean job and lived *out there*, Fanny felt, the world would be safe and lovely.

Imagine, then, Fanny's reaction to the grandeur of New York beheld on a summer's night through the windows of a Greyhound bus whose belly held all her personal possessions. Nature itself was dimmed by that glittering power.

You must understand that Fanny was still a country person. When rain fell against the window of her room in the woman's hotel in midtown Manhattan she did not conceive of it as a front moving across a TV screen or as a maze of shining wet streets and gutters choked with soggy refuse, but as a gift from the country, a matter of shimmer and sound that recalled the tin roof of the little green house and the harmony of raindrops shaking the leaves on the cherry tree outside her window. The city did not cure her grief for the loss of that initial paradise.

But at the beginning her thoughts were mostly on the thrilling new world, the stone forests through which she made her miniature way, the multi-tongued pedestrians in silks and denims. Listening to the excited ticktock of her own heart, she saw the beggars and the homeless mainly as one more colorful element of the general population.

Fanny had heard rumors of the city during her four years at a small Midwestern college, rumors from classmates that led her to apply for an internship at a nationally known publishing house. To her great surprise, she got the internship. On her first day at work, a precise-looking man with circumflex eyebrows called her his young friend as he handed her a sheaf of papers, and the woman for whom she was to work took her to lunch at a Greek restaurant, where she drank white wine and ate rice wrapped in grape leaves. "You're our only intern this year," Mrs. Costard said. "Work hard and they'll spoil you a little."

The lobby of the publisher's building was of a stone that Fanny believed to be marble. Its high oval arches were decorated with stone garlands and benign gargoyles. The publishing house inhabited several floors. Its pale gray corridors were trimmed in white. Chrome and glass tables enlivened the elevator alcoves. A young woman not much older than Fanny worked in the cubicle next to hers. She wore tailored clothes with silky blouses that enhanced her wide-set gray eyes. Her hair was a glossy brown with a slightly flyaway look that, Fanny was to learn, was achieved with some difficulty at a salon tucked away in someone's private residence in the East Eighties. Audrey had graduated from Vassar after spending her junior year at the Sorbonne. She spoke beautiful French, or at least Fanny thought so when Audrey invited Fanny to lunch in a tiny French restaurant. Audrey asked Fanny about her own accent, and Fanny replied that she was a Kentuckian. Audrey was the first New York person to whom Fanny announced what to her was a momentous fact. It turned out that Audrey had once spent a summer in Lexington visiting a cousin and had taken riding lessons at the Horse Park. "Those gorgeous steeds," she said in her lazy, mock-flippant way. "Jeanine and I would go along the fence and slip them sugar cubes." Once Audrey and her cousin had gone east and south along the Mountain Parkway that led into Fanny's hills, when the locust trees were in bloom. "Gorgeous," Audrey said. "How could you bear to leave it?"

Not knowing how to tell the truth in twenty-five words or less, Fanny was tongue-tied. Her shyness made Audrey kind, while Fanny envied Audrey her easy camaraderie with well-groomed young men, editors and writers who had gone to Harvard or to Brown. Fanny was quick to realize that she herself, with her unfashionableness and her grave shyness, was an unlikely candidate for these young men's attentions. But someday, she felt, someday she would learn to be as attractive as Audrey, as fluent in French, as charmingly friendly.

For now, she observed with the same intentness that as

a survivor and oldest child, she had bent upon her youngest brother's frantic efforts to crawl beyond her reach and stick his hand in the lawnmower, upon her sister's arm as she wrestled it free from the old Maytag wringers, and, more sweetly, upon her mother's hands hollowing a bowl in the flour to work the biscuit dough, upon her father's unerring straight rows as he plowed the garden: this same intentness, now, she lavished upon the daily life at the publishing house. Unlike her family, they paid her scant attention in return.

Fanny herself paid little attention to the shabby hotel in which she was sequestered after dark. She did not really notice the shabby clothes of its inhabitants, the meager dinners that many of them consumed in the hotel cafeteria. Mostly these were older women with tired eyes and rounded backs. Fanny sat in her room, her one window open against the city's concrete heat, and read the latest novels praised by the New York Times Sunday Book Review (a habit learned from Audrey) and dreamed, both waking and sleeping.

A man approached her in a cafeteria. He did not resemble the likable boys she had dated in college but was older and more intense. He said he was an actor working as a waiter, but something in the way he said this made Fanny wonder if he was lying. He took her to the Village to a dark bar with loud music. At his instruction, she drank two gin and tonics and let him impersonally and frantically touch her until she became both aroused and repelled. Going home in the subway, she told him to leave her alone, and he called her a frigid bitch. He left the train two stops early, and she continued alone. It was three in the morning and all the bourgeois had gone home except for a bunch of drunken boys in the next car. She got off at her stop and ran.

At the publishing house, Fanny was doing well. She was an excellent proofreader and often caught small editing mistakes. One day she wrote a few paragraphs about an incident she had witnessed on the subway. A man with whisky breath led his fox terrier into the car, and, at his prodding, the sad-eyed little dog begged prettily up and down the aisle. Several people dropped money in the man's hat and smiled and looked at each other. Fanny had simultaneously a sense of home and a wave of homesickness, but she did not say so in the article she wrote. Mrs. Costard read it and said that no, it wouldn't do for the *Times*, say, but keep on trying. "You're a hard worker," she said and patted Fanny's shoulder. Fanny knew that a permanent job might open up in a few weeks, and she began to hope.

She longed to make the acquaintance of the skinny Asian-looking man whose desk was piled high with books on painting and calligraphy, of the robust woman who hummed complicated music as she sped down the hall, of the young black woman who looked exotic and extremely intelligent. Sometimes she did find herself in conversation with an interesting-looking person, but her own reticence helped keep these dialogues lifeless. She never mentioned Kentucky, protecting her memories of the first home like a beautiful but fragile secret. One slip of the tongue might make her seem incapable of belonging. Kentucky was beautiful, but as an exiled hillbilly, she was ungainly and unsightly. In the Midwestern college she had belonged to a rebellious marginal group, but the city was paradise and she wanted to belong to its inner realms. She was frightened and distressed when she experienced a growing anger against the perfunctoriness that marked her social day.

Anderson began to give her an intimate little wave as he went past her office. Anderson had curly hair with reddish glints in it and broad, expressive shoulders. His dark eyes were clever and quick. He spoke with the broad A's that befitted his Bostonian background. Fanny knew she was one of several women to whom Anderson waved, and she felt flattered to be included.

If she got a real job, she could get an apartment and buy the Julia Child paperback she had seen in bookstore windows. She would take French lessons at the New School. She would go to Audrey's hairdresser. Surely, in the long run, such things would accumulate and compensate for the fact that she had not gone to summer camp, for the fact that she had never been abroad, for the fact that her parents hadn't gone beyond the eighth grade, and so forth. Clearly, a certain anxiety had begun to cloud Fanny's visions of paradise, but she felt that it was merely a matter of refashioning herself, of developing, so to speak, angelic habits.

In mid-June, Audrey invited Fanny to spend the long weekend of the Fourth at her family's Long Island home. Fanny was thrilled and frightened. She was at the same time homesick. Her mother wrote her that the family, who had moved back to Kentucky, where her father now had a precarious job, were having a picnic at Cumberland Lake in southeastern Kentucky. The family had been there once several years before when Fanny was still at home. She pictured the wide, deep lake with its glittering geodes spilled along the rocky beaches, the high green depths of the mountains that surrounded it. She saw her mother's broad, comely face with its brown eyes so like her own. She saw her father's curly black hair as he bent over a canoe to make sure it was lakeworthy. She saw her siblings, for whom she had once been a second mother, oohing and ahing over the geodes, as she herself would like to do. Had she had enough money, she would have gone home for the Fourth, though it would have been with deep, anxious regret that she turned down Audrey's invitation. As it was, she accepted it gladly and worried for two weeks about what to pack for such a weekend. Bring a swimsuit, Audrey said, so she restricted herself to tuna sandwiches for dinner and bought a black two-piece number that she had seen at Bloomingdale's.

As they drew near the village on the fringe of which Audrey's family lived, on a clear Saturday morning with sea salt in the air, and sometimes in a far corner the blue secret ocean, Fanny pressed her nose against the window of Audrey's Honda Civic and grew increasingly nervous. They had left behind dreary miles of overpopulated towns with what seemed to be the same motel on the outskirts of each. Now tree-bracketed driveways hid large houses whose gabled roofs were barely visible. The village itself was a chain of shops in fake Victorian buildings. The pharmacy advertised its fountain, which Audrey said had become a campy place to hang out. "They put the fountain in last year," she said. "It's the authentic village look, don't you think?"

It looked very pretty and elegant, Fanny thought. The whole village did. She recognized the name of a well-known manicure chain on one of the shops and looked quickly at her fingernails to make sure they were well-shaped and clean.

Beyond the village they turned into one of many drive-ways. The tree-lined lane opened up suddenly into a broad gravel path flanked by multicolored flower beds. The gray stone house was large, though not so palace-like as Fanny had imagined. Two long-haired dogs with floppy ears came running to greet Audrey. "That's Dindie," she said, "and this one's Danmont." A sharp-featured woman whose eyes were like Audrey's met them in the hall. She hugged Audrey perfunctorily and said to the man behind her, "and here's Audrey's little friend." To Audrey she said, "Mary's mother is ill, so I had to give her the weekend off. She would have quit if I hadn't." "And here's Daddy," Audrey said and went past her mother to hug him. He was a large, balding man with kind eyes. Fanny knew that he was the president of a communications company, so she looked at him with great curiosity. "How's my girl," he asked Audrey.

"Bring your friend out on the terrace after you get settled in," Mrs. Elland said. "We're having lunch on the terrace." She had pale dense skin and blonde hair, and she was as trim-figured as Audrey.

"Your mother has pretty hair," Fanny told Audrey as they walked up the wide, carpeted stairs, past violent abstract paintings at which Audrey stuck out her tongue. "Mother's support-your-local-artist period," she said. "As for her hair, only her hairdresser knows for sure. And me. And now you."

Fanny laughed nervously.

The guestroom was wallpapered, reminding Fanny of her bedroom in the Kentucky home and of her mother, who had mixed flour and water paste and sweatily smoothed on the strips of paper, taking infinite care to match each panel. The soft-looking bed was covered with a white comforter. A wrought-iron table beside it carried a row of paperback mysteries. "My choice," Audrey said, touching the books. A glass vase on the bureau held red and white gladioli. "What a great room," Fanny said, wincing at her own predicta-bility, but it was true. "I'll say this for my mother," Audrey answered. "She's got great taste in interior decorators."

Shocked from her instinctive reticence by Audrey's tone of voice, Fanny blurted, "Don't you like your mother?"

Audrey looked away. "Don't get me wrong," she said. "I love my mother. But I don't like her very much."

"Why?"

"It's a long story I'll tell you sometime," Audrey replied. "Can't tell you all the family secrets on the first day," she added flippantly and turned toward the door. "There are fresh towels in your bathroom. I'll pick you up on my way downstairs."

Fanny looked out the window at a long green lawn dotted with large-branched trees that cast a purple shade in the noonday sun. She wondered if she should change clothes, as people did in novels.

The terrace overlooked a stone-lined pond that turned out to be the swimming pool. A pitcher of lemonade sat on a round table with small sandwiches and fruit. Mr. Elland was pouring something clear with ice and fruit in it from another pitcher that sat on the bench beside his chair.

"Oh, Mother's white sangria," Audrey said. "Come on, Dad, give. And let Fanny have one, too."

Her father obligingly got two glasses from the table and poured from the second pitcher. "Best thing your mother makes," he said.

"Remember what I told you when you proposed," his wife said. The flippancy in her voice reminded Fanny of Audrey. "I don't cook and I don't do windows."

Mr. Elland laughed as though at a joke that he had heard too often.

"My mother comes from a long line of servant-bearing families," Audrey said slyly. "But Daddy is a self-made man."

"From the ground up," he said, lifting his glass. "You're from Kentucky, aren't you?" he asked Fanny. "My brother lived in Lexington for years, in one of those old Federal houses. He was very proud of it."

"I've never been to Lexington," Fanny said apologetically.

"Fanny's from the hills," Audrey said.

"Ah. What does your father do there?"

"He works in the mines," Fanny said. She felt that if Mr. Elland looked down her throat, he would see a whole world sticking there.

"What does he do in the mines?" he asked curiously, looking at Mrs. Elland.

"He's a mine electrician."

"I'm sure he's very good at it," Mrs. Elland said.

"Oh, he is." Fanny wanted suddenly, urgently, to talk. To tell someone about her parents, her siblings, her grandmother, her aunts and uncles and cousins.

Mr. Elland poured himself another glass of sangria. "Saw the funniest thing in the City yesterday," he said, settling back. "In Grand Central. There was a bag lady in the waiting room. Don't ask me how she eluded the police, but there she was, in seven layers of dirty clothes, I'm sure, and two laundry sacks of god knows what setting in front of her. And on her head was a *huge* picture hat, you know," he said, turning to Mrs. Elland, "the kind Greta Garbo or Joan Crawford used to wear. Some old guy sat down beside her, and she took out the longest hat pin I ever saw and pricked his arm." Mr. Elland threw back his head and laughed, and Mrs. Elland joined him. Fanny felt a sudden, unwanted protectiveness toward the bag lady. Head down so that they might not notice she was not laughing, she remembered her own indifference to the beggars and homeless on Manhattan's streets. She noticed that Audrey did not laugh.

Mrs. Elland turned to Audrey. "I saw Jack Winterford in the village last week. They're here for the summer."

"Is Nell with them?"

"No. Maury got his marine biologist position at Wood's Hole. She's going to have a baby, too."

"I miss Nell," Audrey said. "The old Nell. We were going to burn a lot of bridges together."

"You've burned enough bridges," her father said sharply.

Talk turned to the publishing house, and Audrey told funny anecdotes about people that Fanny wouldn't have dared joke about, though she laughed uneasily and corroborated her new friend. For she saw in some way now that she and Audrey were indeed friends. A new sensation attended that friendship, one which she would never have expected to have. She felt sorry for Audrey, whom she understood to be doing battle against her parents and perhaps losing the battle.

There was a pause in the conversation. "Your brother's coming here tomorrow," Mr. Elland said to his daughter.

Audrey looked at him. "I'm glad. How long is he staying?"

"Only until Monday afternoon. They're renovating his room at the school."

Fanny had never heard Audrey mention a brother.

Later, when they had put on their swimming suits and were lazing in the pool, Audrey said, "My brother's severely retarded. His name is Arthur."

"Oh, I'm sorry," Fanny stuttered.

Mrs. Elland bought an excellent dinner from a nearby restaurant and served it by candlelight. Mr. Elland brought out the family photo albums and showed Fanny pictures of

Audrey as a four-year-old ballet star.

Upstairs that evening, Audrey, saying goodnight, said suddenly. "Daddy wasn't being cruel about the bag lady. It's just that it was *funny*. He always gives them money."

"It's okay," Fanny reassured her new friend, but some part of her felt that it wasn't okay.

Fanny slept well in the guestroom. After spending half an hour sitting in the dark in the armchair by the window and watching the dim harmonies of trees in a slight wind, she read a Michael Innes mystery and dropped off to sleep without letting herself think about anything.

In the morning, when she went downstairs, the others were sitting in the blue-checkered and copper-urned breakfast nook beside the greenhouse. She looked for Audrey's brother.

Audrey said, looking at her mother, "Arthur's not here. He's staying at the local hospital until his room is renovated. And Fanny and I are leaving after breakfast." Mrs. Elland got up and stalked into the house.

"Audrey," her father said.

"You don't care," his daughter cried.

Breakfast—walnut pancakes with maple syrup and dark aromatic coffee—was eaten in silence.

Audrey shut the door behind them as her father brought the Honda from the three-car garage. "I'm sorry, baby," he said softly, and Audrey whispered, "Not good enough, Dad."

Then they were on the road back.

"I heard you were going to get that job," Audrey said. "I was saving the news until the fireworks tonight. Sorry, Fanny, I'm really sorry."

Fanny told her friend not to be silly, there was nothing to be sorry about. They drove on quietly. Fanny pressed her nose against the window to catch the blue secrets of the ocean as she mourned the loss of paradise. Probably she would take the job if it were offered to her, but in her heart, she knew now what she had suspected for some time: that the years ahead would be long and difficult and that the way back was just as uncharted and could be reached only by going forward.

Tecumseh

It was a fall day in central Ohio, soft, cool, the kind of day when God, if he existed, looked like a great artist. She surreptitiously scuffed satisfyingly noisy leaves with her sensible shoes. Her husband, now fifty, said, "By God, lady, sometimes you're still a child." Once he would have said this teasingly, but now he sounded tired and flat. Sally Anslip sighed. Hard years had pitted the sanguine disposition she had acquired as a petted child, her cheeriness honed to a luminous hope. Men found her touching, always feeling that she was shorter than them and slightly fragile—even her husband and sons, who had had occasion to respect her robust practicality and tensile strength.

Forrest was out of work now that Dr. Pruitt had sold the farm. Sally thought, walking beside her stooped husband, that Forrest's back would soon have made it impossible for him to continue managing the farm anyhow, since, manager or no, he had to get down on his knees in the brown/black soil, and he had to spray the pear and apple and plum trees and tend the black-and-white Holsteins that Dr. Pruitt was fanatic about.

"What are we going to do without the farm?" the doctor had said woefully, fumbling with his thick-rimmed glasses and then mussing his thick white hair wildly in the way he had when he was disturbed. He put down the pitcher of iced tea they had been sharing in the backyard. The two men shook their heads forebodingly while Sally watched silently behind the screen door. It was her iced tea. You put eight bags of decaf tea in a small amount of boiled water and let it set for thirty-five minutes. Then you squeezed the teabags and discarded them, added two-thirds cup of sugar, put the tea water in the blue pitcher, and filled it to the brim. The children always asked her to make her tea "Our Southern tea," Nicole, who had had a scholarship to Oberlin College, would say archly, fluffing her short reddish-brown hair. Her mother always wondered if her daughter's name, which had belonged to a book Sally had been reading at the time—she no longer remembered the title or the contents of the book—had led to her daughter's being so uppity about her home.

Anson and Scott, named for Forrest and Sally's fathers, were much more down-to-earth. They had remained close to home, while Nicole had moved away to New York City, where she worked for an advertising agency. Anson, who was in the kitchen now, had a small farm. Today he had left his busy wife at home and traveled the ten miles between his farm and their street in Latchett to help his father clean the gutters and remove branches from the backyard. There had been a frightening storm over the weekend, with seventy-mile-an-hour winds punctuated by fierce lightning. As always, she had worried about the big old sycamore in the backyard, but it had held, minus a limb and a lot of shabby bark. Anson's brother, who worked for the electric company, was out on the line somewhere, Sally guessed. Thousands of central Ohioans were without power. Even at other times, the power people rarely seemed to be able to spare him. This second, silent son showed up for the big celebrations but was otherwise always occupied elsewhere. Maybe, after all, he was not down to earth. (She had a quick vision of her son as an angel perched on an electric pole. No angel, Scott.) He certainly couldn't forever be working at his job. What did he do on the other side of town that prevented him from spending more time with his family?

Nicole got home about three times a year: Fourth of July weekend, Thanksgiving, Christmas. Independence Day, they had a picnic with grilled burgers and hotdogs and Sally's cake that looked like an American flag, and Scott bought fireworks and set them off in the backyard. Although you could buy great fireworks in Ohio, it was not legal to set them off, a contradiction that Forrest and all the children scoffed at. Always as the bright-hued showers shot up and away, Sally kept expecting the sheriff to turn up and throw the lot of them in jail. Or was it the state police?

Nicole came in November partly because her grandparents on her mother's side and her father's sister Olivia and several cousins from both sides would come for Thanksgiving Dinner. When she could get away, she would arrive a week early and help clean the house and do the baking. Christmas she came because they all loved the family Christmas. Even Scott. Christmas, with sweets and meats and sodas and tinsel and glass and the smell of the cedar tree that Forrest always brought in and the small presents, the dolls, the balls, the cap guns, had seemed like a season of paradise during those years when money was really short. Sally sometimes wondered if the fact that her children still loved Christmas at home meant that they were having rough lives out there.

She heard Dr. Pruitt say, "Well, now, Forrest, then, I got a proposition for you. You know my other farm, over in Licking County—the little market I got attached to it. My store manager is retiring in six weeks, and I could sure use you and Sally to mind that store—make the sales, make sure the produce is fresh, you know. You're at least ten years younger than Birkett is, and my son Nick will see that the place gets cleaned and that kind of thing." Sally fancied she saw a gleam of interest in her husband's eye. "It honestly wouldn't be that much work," the doctor continued, "but I could sure use somebody I could trust. There's a house for you to live in, a pretty nice one if I do say so myself. Market's been there for thirty years now, looking solid. And the farm does nicely and will do even better now that I can put the resources I had in this one over there." Sally and Forrest knew the store manager and his wife. They had been in the pretty nice house, and it was pretty nice. Sally felt a sharp distress.

"Aaiih, I don't know," Forrest answered, plucking at his arm hairs in the way he always did when he was stressed. They had left it at that, Forrest promising to think it over. Sally felt that that was what he was doing on their walk, and she knew a quick anger that he was not discussing it with her. She stopped abruptly and turned to look toward the street where their house was, its steep green roof showing above the intervening structures, smack in the middle of

Broad Street. On one side, Sally's cousin Alastair lived, a jovial sweet man, lawyer (family trusts and wills), who knew everybody in town and who brought half the world over to see the Anslips. On the other side were the Darbys, man and wife, who kept to themselves most of the month and then, on the last Saturday, usually, invited their neighbors over for coffee and cake. The Anslip house, which everybody called the old Church place, was a white-painted brick house with dark green shutters and a tall cedar tree in the narrow front yard. What was the word Nicole liked to use? Provenance. It had provenance. It had been built soon after the Spanish-American War by a local architect who had won awards for his public buildings in the state. He had intended to live there with his second wife and second brood of children but had died of a heart attack the day the family was scheduled to move in. There was a portrait of him in the Latchett Public Library: pale, driven, handsome, with a shock of wavy black hair. His brother, who afterward became a judge, had moved in instead, and for eighty years, some of Latchett's leading citizens had lived in that house. A doctor in the 1920s had painted the brick white, a look which the Church family considered so elegant that no one had ever changed back to the original red. Sally was that doctor's granddaughter. Her mother had inherited the house from a brother, Ray (she was his favorite sister), and had given the house to Sally in time of need.

Sally's mother had married a young east Kentuckian greatly to the disappointment of her own mother, who forbade the wedding. The young woman had eloped with her miner, who had been in Latchett visiting an elementary school teacher, formerly of Kentucky, who had taught Uncle Ray. Ray, who was then still living at home, had invited the

Kentuckian to dinner, where Sally's mother-to-be was present.

And Ray was the only relative present at his sister's brief wedding ceremony, having been in on the flight from its inception. Marie Church of Latchett, Ohio, had become the bride of Scott Mercer of Green Branch, Kentucky (Osier County). On Green Branch (a tributary of the Big Muddy), she ruined her white town hands—her poor Ohio hands, her doting husband would say, stroking them as they sat on the front porch watching a mountain night swallow the valley floor and then living things and then the hills—working in the large garden and cornfield of their small farm while he delved in the dark, damp mine in which his father had died. In the evenings when Scott Mercer came home he did whatever plowing and fixing and remaining cornfield hoeing needed to be done. Sally remembered that her parents had quarreled occasionally, usually when she resented his intermittent authoritarianism or when he resented her town ladidahs, as he called them—but they had been content on the whole, their daughter believed. Their seven children had arrived without undue incident. Sally, born in 1958, was the youngest.

She had been a bright girl, valedictorian of Green Branch High School, in a graduating class of twenty-five. That was two years after the mine had laid Scott Mercer off as its owners switched more and more to machines. "I'm happy they did," Sally's mother scolded. "Your father can't take that going under the ground anymore." It was true that he had become increasingly querulous and bent and cough-prone and also true that he now joined his younger brother in doing farm work, where he acted like a man reprieved. But money was low. The winter before Sally's graduation, the only meat they had was some canned pork that Marie had put up from the November slaughter of their last hog. It had run out in March. The children—except the very oldest son, who had died in flames in Vietnam and was buried, what scraps of him graced the coffin, at the foot of Sarvis Mountain—tried to help but other than Sally, still in school, and Ricky, on the farm, they had families of their own. So Sally had had to make do with a re-hemmed hand-me-down from her sister June for a graduation dress. But it was a pretty, rose-colored dress, and Sally was sanguine if occasionally a little hungry. Forrest Anslip, who would be in the audience, had never seen the dress on *her*.

Marie had hoped that Sally would get a scholarship and go away to college in Ohio, maybe Ohio State University, and become a teacher, but Sally would not leave Green Branch. She liked her life crowded with aunts and uncles and cousins, and she was being courted by Forrest Anslip, a fine figure of a man (as Sally's closest friend, who was a bookworm, said) with hazel eyes and dark hair. With the moral offered by their own marriage, the Mercers did not forbid Sally's when she insisted but entered into its details with a kind of joyous abandon, leaving the future to the future. As for Sally, she was completely taken with this awkward man with the vulnerable eyes and the broad hands that were so uncertain in rest position, so sure and skilled when they were occupied. She loved to touch his hard right arm, with its scar from a barbed-wire fencing incident, and she loved to run her fingers through the silky ink of his hair. She remembered wrestling with him when they were six. Their families had attended the same hillside Baptist church.

Although the two of them paid little attention to religious matters, they paid tribute to their families' tradition and did not go to bed before the wedding. The young woman of eighteen was scared and then ecstatic on her wedding night (though fleetingly jealous of her husband's obvious experience). Such a flood she had not expected. It took months for her to integrate this delightful new experience into anything like a sensible approach to life. The death of her first child after three months of pregnancy would accomplish the next level of knowledge, that and Forrest's mine injury that crushed his left thumb, plus the return of Forrest's crotchety father and unhappy mother from a long visit to their daughter in Indiana. (At the time, Forrest and Sally were living in his parents' two-story house while they hunted for a decent place they could afford.)

To his wife, Forrest did not seem to belong to either of his parents; he was strong and often pleased with life. Other young miners would come to seek his advice and invite him to play softball with them or to bring his new wife to a family picnic. When Ricky hurt his leg on the tractor, it was Forrest who took him to the hospital and who came back and finished baling hay for him. When Sally was in bed with her pregnancy, he learned how to cook, after a fashion, and he did the dishes and the laundry. "Well, you're just too good to be true, Forrest Anslip," she said teasingly one day a month after the unborn baby's death as she began to feel human again, even with an empty space inside her, and when he flushed, "but I won't tell on you." (They did not make love again for several months, and when they finally did their passion was muted, although it sometimes became a kind of tender delight. "Are you okay?" he asked anxiously the first few times, and she felt the separation that fear and loss had caused, and she grieved again.)

They finally found a place on Rusty Creek, which ran into Green Branch. The two streams met at the foot of Mayapple Hill, whose rotund tree-laced bulge shadowed the juncture, the deep cool hole where the Mercers and the An-slips and other families would swim late spring, summer, early fall. It was at this swimming hole that they had wrestled as six-year-olds after he threw what she considered to be too much water on her brother and her. East of May-apple, in a nook half in sunshine, half in shade, their new house was a long, black-tarred log house, not an old log cabin but a snug, modern affair, a railroad house, the two bedrooms in single file behind the large living room and the kitchen tacked on at the other end. The owner was an older miner who liked Forrest and gave them a long-standing option to buy. A roomy garden sat to its left and a small orchard to its right. Behind there was a chicken house. They thought they would want to buy. "Maybe in two or three years," Forrest said, "and maybe we can buy the bottomland across the road." How fortunate they were to find a house on a broad valley floor with huckleberry mountains on either side.

The older Sally in Latchett still remembered her husband's declaration during their first night of occupancy. "You bring me good luck," he had whispered ecstatically, and she had felt deeply treasured at the ordinary words, a feeling that had fed her marriage like an underground spring up until three weeks ago. She remembered too another, later scene in the spacious living room of that house which they had loved. There had been a methane explosion at the mine, and three miners were dead, seven badly injured. The word was that the mine had been paying off the state inspectors and ignoring safety precautions. Twenty miners had crowded into their living room, and her husband like a young bear had been the focal point of the meeting. They wanted him to be the official whistleblower. "They'll listen to you," one of the older miners said. "We'll back you up." Forrest threw a look in Sally's direction, but he agreed to act without consulting her. The young wife had been so proud of her husband that she easily buried her anger, though not her misgivings. Ray, who was visiting them, whispered to his niece, "He's like a young Tecumseh." In school, Ray had made a study of Tecumseh, the Shawnee Indian chief who had tried so hard to preserve the tribes from the white man's greed. His niece knew that for him to say this was in part the kind of exaggeration that families go in for but was nonetheless a mark of respect and affection. Afterward, at all moments when she was particularly proud of her husband, she secretly called him "Tecumseh."

In the desultory conversations that followed, the same older miner who had urged Forrest on said, "Did you all hear that the space shuttle, they call it, flew on its own today. They'll never get it on up to the moon."

"I don't like the idea of its being up there, suspended over our heads," another man said. "It'll crash, and some people are going to get hurt."

Forrest shook his head. "The Enterprise is just a beginning to it," he said. "Like all of the space program is just beginning. Our grandchildren may go to Mars or Venus as easy as those guys reached the moon." Forrest read newspapers. He always went to Osierville on Sundays and bought the *Lexington Herald* and the *Osierville Examiner*. He still spoke to Sally with awe about watching the first moon landing on the high school TV.

In later years, after they had left Osier County, Sally was to connect this image of her young husband, her Tecumseh, standing there sure of himself and respected by his fellows, with her own childhood, the lost days of paradise. Forrest had lost his job and been blacklisted by the other mines there about. Now it was Sally and Forrest who had no money. The owner of the log house let them stay six months without paying rent, but then his wife needed an operation, and he had to ask them to leave. Pretending that he was a farmer who had no previous mining experience, Forrest found a job in West Virginia, and they had moved to a coal camp with a slag mountain across the railroad that ran in front of their house and a greasy river down under the steep bank that lay at the back. To their house's left was a noisy family. The husband worked the evening shift, and when he came in late at night, the whole lot of them seemed to be up and about, making a racket. Forrest finally complained, but the only result was that the mother considered this a social overture and would come to visit, bringing her four children and spending the afternoon. Sally liked her but got tired of her company. On the other side there was a bleak field strewn with garbage.

Nicole was born there, a difficult delivery. Sally had lost a lot of blood and required transfusions. She and the baby stayed in the hospital for ten days. "Thank god for the insurance," she said to Forrest during late visiting hours. He could not come during the day when he was working. She lay in the clean white hospital bed, nursing her baby when she was brought to her and crying at other times and plotting how to get out of their current life. "We can't bring her up in this place," she told her husband, and he shook his head in agreement. He started looking for another job. "It's been a year," he said. "I'll find some good excuse to move on." But work was scarce in the mines just then.

They started making weekend excursions into the countryside, looking for a house. Living in the coal camp, Sally had not appreciated how lovely the West Virginia landscape could be. There was as yet no mountaintop removal mining in that particular area and not much strip mining. The mountains rolled on every side like great green breakers with a froth of rhododendron. On the Easter after Nicole's birth, they picnicked at the top of Horseshoe Mountain, in a mossy green clearing beneath gigantic trees, the sun thudding down like a spring heartbeat. Sally looked into the stern recesses of the forest and regretted the gentler slopes of home at the same time that she was lyrically moved by the impending mountain. They saw a farm at the foot of the mountain, not much of a farm but with outbuildings and a good-sized garden. "Too bad it's too far from work," Forrest sighed.

Eventually, they found a place to live, about ten miles east of the coal camp: about five acres of bumpy flatland, surrounded on all sides by a larger farm. It had been rented by the farmer's son, who decided to move into town and start up a car repair place. The farmer shook his head. "He may be back, you know," he said honestly to his would-be renters. "This ain't the best time to be starting a business around here." They were young, and they figured that by the time the son's business might fail they would be ready to move on, perhaps even back home. The son's business *had* failed, two years later, but he chose to move on himself to the state of Washington.

The soil was not that good, and the house was ramshackle. Forrest repaired the roof and fixed the windows, and they painted their five-room home inside and out. They built a chicken coop. The house was heated only by a coal-burning grate in the living room and a coal stove in the kitchen. That winter, they froze upstairs, and alternately scorched their faces and their backsides downstairs. At Christmas, they bought space heaters for the bedrooms as their presents to each other. Santa Claus came for Nicole and left a doll and a tea set under the pretty cedar Forrest had cut on a nearby mountainside. "I wonder whose property it is," Sally said, and Forrest answered, "I was too busy getting myself out of there to wonder about *that!*" The mine gave them a turkey for Christmas dinner, and Sally baked apple pies and chocolate cake. Santa gave them all chocolate candy and, traditionally, an apple and an orange and, for the grownups, lots of nuts. Sally grieved for her absent family. In February, they went home, a ritual they were to repeat twice a year for most of their seventeen years in West Virginia. Once in a long while, someone would come to visit them.

That first spring, they bought baby chicks by mail, and Forrest rigged up a heating lamp for the downy bits of fluff, several of whom died from some unknown disease and ten of whom were murdered by a fox. The farmer sold Forrest a cow: a Jersey, and her calf. She was giving so much milk they had plenty, even with the calf taking its share. Sally loved the rich Jersey cream, much of which she made into a heavenly butter, using the churn Marie had given her as a wedding present. It had belonged to her great-grandmother. Forrest made a new wooden dasher for it. Like the chicks, the calf was adorable, and Sally named it Red-ear because it had one red ear (the other one was white). Later they would sell the calf for beef, but in the meantime, she saw no reason not to love it. She had grown up with farm animals. What she could not bring herself to do was kill a chicken for Sunday dinner. Forrest did that, and later, Anson. Forrest fixed the fence around the garden and fertilized the soil with manure he got from the farmer, and they planted beans, tomatoes, peas, cucumbers, muskmelons, watermelons, peppers, potatoes, corn, and okra. The soil wasn't right for sweet potatoes.

But the place never really seemed like home. However,

Nicole was healthy, and soon Anson was born, and five years later, Scott. They were all lonely, even Forrest, who had buddies at the mine. She wondered if they should go to church but was enough of a believer to feel guilty about treating church as a social venue. The farmer's wife and grown daughter would stop on their way to town and spend a while. They were friendly enough but always aware that they were owners while Sally was a renter. And there were no other young children around. She had just about made up her mind to ask Forrest to take them to church when one day one of his mine buddies came to visit and brought along his wife, a peroxide blonde with dark roots showing. She wore heavy mascara and bright red lipstick. These things did not bother Sally nearly so much as her speech. "Well, honey, I says to him, if you want to keep me home you'd better be bringing home the bacon instead of spending it on that poker game. There's plenty of men down at Joe's Bar be glad to give me the time of day. He hit me then, and I hit him right back. Well, you got to know, I was mad because he promised to get me a new coat and he gambled it away. Anyhow, we kissed and made up all right. Uh-huh, didn't we?" After they left, Forrest said apologetically, "He's a good man in a pinch, but he's got no taste in women. I don't doubt she hooked him with that pretty face." Sally, who wore no makeup, wondered if she should get some mascara and lipstick.

So it went until the two older children began to go to school. Even though, according to the farmer's wife, the school had a reputation for wildness, Nicole and Anson managed to find steady friends. Nicole was befriended by a teacher's daughter who also liked to read. From time to time, Angela's father would bring her over to play with Nicole, saying a friendly but distant hello to Sally. Forrest was always at work when they came.

One day Nicole came in crying. "That bully slapped me," she sobbed. "He said I was stuck-up because I was friends with Angie, and I slapped him, and he slapped me back." Forrest went to school with her the next day, made her point out the bully, and talked to the boy. Sally was afraid that would make matters worse, but it didn't. "Don't do that again, though," she said to her husband. "They could gang up on her." "Aiaah, the boy wasn't that bad," Forrest said. "Just jealous of Nicole and showing off to his friends a little. Our daughter's right smart in school, her teacher says. She shouldn't have slapped him." Sally noticed that Nicole at play with Angela tended to tag along behind, and she noticed later that Angela's friends became Nicole's friends rather than the other way around.

Anson took up with the popular kids in his class. Forrest delivered him to play basketball and baseball, and he did well at the games, making himself popular, too. He had something of Forrest's easy assurance with other males. His friends listened to him. He was shy around girls.

When Scott's time for schooling came, he was not easy. He hung out with rough children from the coal camp, learning how to curse and be rude to adults. Anson's friends were coal camp kids too, Forrest pointed out. But the camp had its wild element (among adults as well as children). In the sixth grade, the teacher caught Scott and another boy and a girl smoking marijuana. One of them pointed out the older boy who had sold the reefers to them—not Scott, though. He refused to tell, even after Forrest, as a last resort, whipped him with a belt. The boy turned sullen and unresponsive at home, and they could do nothing with him for a while. But in the eighth grade, a charismatic new teacher took an interest in him and his friends, singling Scott out as a bright kid with interest in mathematics and getting him interested in music, teaching him to play the flute. Sally, turning thankful eyes on her son's teacher, could hardly believe the delicate sounds issuing from her turbulent son. When she reached out to him, though, he answered her politely now but backed away. Forrest treated him with tact, but there was little emotion expressed between them. Scott's allegiances lay elsewhere.

They had bought a color TV, and one night Sally, who rarely watched the box although the rest of her family were mesmerized by it for the first year or so, saw Thornton Wilder's "The Skin of Our Teeth." Its portrayal of the tribulations of ordinary people moved her deeply. The next time they went to the library, she checked out the two Wilder books on the shelf. Forrest had also watched the drama, and he laughed and sighed as well. Both his laughter and his sighs were stronger than those of his wife. Sally looked over at her husband. She had not looked at him as a separate entity for some time. His dark hair had patches of silver, she saw, and his hazel eyes were, as always, rimmed with coal dust. There went two deep wrinkles in his forehead and a burn scar (mining accident) beside his mouth. His nails were thick and bent, and his smashed thumb from the old injury marred his right hand. Once in a while, he suffered a paroxysm of harsh coughing. One night during their tenth year in West Virginia, she had found him standing at the edge of the garden staring bleakly into space. "What's wrong, Forrest?" she asked anxiously. "It's the union," he said without turning to look at her. "They want me to run for office." She thought forebodingly about his whistle-blowing back home, but seeing his unhappiness, said anyway, "Why don't you?" "They might find out I lied about working in the mines at home," he said. "I could lose my job." Still staring into the dark, he said, "Sally, I'm sick of going down into the dark, but I don't know what else to do."

He began to work tirelessly on their five acres, scrubbing it up, his wife thought, until it shone in the sun. He worked until the sun went down most days. They both worked hard, and so did the children. The garden full of vegetables, the yard full of flowers, the outbuildings painted, the animals in fine shape. Blueberry bushes so fertile that they were able to sell little boxes of them in town. He set a trap and caught the fox, and then he got out his rifle and got rid of some raccoons and rabbits. When he asked the farmer if he could rent the bottomland lying fallow behind the house, the farmer looked at what he had done and said, "Well, yes, you sure can. I'll get benefit out of it later on." Forrest planted a small orchard, and when Sally chided him, saying, "We probably won't even be here when it bears fruit, and it costs money, Forrest." "You never know," her husband answered, and he carefully tended the trees year after year. They were harvesting Golden Delicious apples on Anson's twelfth birthday and had been eating their Bosc and Bartlett pears for some time. Marie and Scott Senior came that fall and were full of praise for their son-in-law. That evening Marie cried. "You'll never come home," she said to her daughter. Feelings of exile attacked Sally afresh. She knew it was in part loneliness that fed them, but she distrusted the world around her, and she did not drive. It had only recently occurred to her that she could drive if she wanted to, and she thought she would ask Forrest to teach her when he had the time.

That time came sooner than she expected. There was unrest at the mine about safety. Part of a roof had collapsed. Luckily nobody had been working in that section at the time. "Men could have been hurt bad," Forrest said. "Somebody could have been killed. I don't know, lady, we been here a long time and I'm thinking I could join the union now. If somebody don't do something, they're going to do us out of it." "Do you have to be the one?" Sally asked half-angrily—only half because he looked like Ray's Tecumseh when he made the announcement, and she felt some freeing up of their life, a throwing off of yokes. But nevertheless, she said, "Remember back home, Forrest." "I'll be as careful as I can, honey," he said, his face alight. That night they came together in a wordless passion that frightened Sally, as though deluges were no longer safe.

In half a year, somebody had dug up the old information, and Forrest was fired for lying on his application. She learned how to drive. They lost the car. "We sure can't go back home," Forrest said. "I got no work credentials anywhere now." Sally had already figured that out. Seeing their father stay home during the week and look somber, the children worried. "What will Daddy work at now?" Nicole asked her mother anxiously. She was sixteen. There were the children at school, Sally thought, the ones with twice-mended shoes for whom the local churches provided lunch. And the ones back home they saw when they went to visit. Scott Senior had become a carpenter, and Marie sold produce, so her parents eked out a halfway decent living, but there were others who did not, including June's and Simon's families. June's husband had been out of work for two years, and the rest of the family had to help them out. Sally and Forrest had sent a little now and then. Simon had the black lung ailment and was trying to get payments; his wife was a clerk at the hospital, so they managed somehow with their family of seven.

Forrest found an old jalopy for fifty dollars and made it

go. Since he could fix just about anything, he got work here and there. Sally sold produce, like her mother, but winter was coming. They fought over little things. The children fought. She received anxious letters from home—letters from Marie with a postscript from Scott Senior. Sally's parents had managed to hang onto the telephone for Scott Senior's repair services and job searching, and one day Marie called. Nicole, who was moodily hanging around the house (Angela and two friends had invited her to go to the movies with them, but there was no money for movies), answered the phone, and after parrying some questions about how school was going, passed the receiver to Sally. Marie and Sally never called each other unless there was some special reason for it, so Sally asked, "Is everything okay, Mom? You and Dad all right?" Marie reassured her daughter and came quickly to the point, although her voice hesitated and slowed down as she proceeded. "Now don't get upset, Sally, and just listen to what I have to say." Sally agreed anxiously. "You remember your uncle Ray died a couple of years ago?" "Yes, Mommy." "You know he left me the house in Latchett. Well, it's just been sitting there," Marie said defensively, and her voice speeded up, "and there's more jobs in Ohio, and it's a good house, and your Dad and me want you and Forrest to have it."

"We can't do that. It's yours. It's a good nest egg. You could sell it."

"But I don't want to sell it. It's my home. You being there will give me a good excuse to come and visit. And it'll keep the place from falling apart."

Sally felt shame at the prospect of taking, thinking too of her brothers and sisters and what their reaction would be. She pictured the house in Ohio. In childhood they had gone to Latchett at least once a year, and Grandma, who looked so much like Sally, greeted them profusely, her old disapproval of Marie's marriage forgotten with the arrival of children. She would lead them into the rich, mellow kitchen with its sunshine yellow and oak hues and give them freshly baked cookies, scolding them for being absent for so long. "And what about everybody else? What about June and Simon?"

"Simon's got his black lung payments now, and you know Herbert got an electrician's job at the Pocahontas mine back in May, so June and the kids are all right." Marie paused, out of breath, and Sally saw her mother's thin face, with its distinctive cheekbones, her lips puckered with her effort to persuade. With a rush of exhaled air, Marie continued: "Anyway, nobody here at home wants to move to Ohio." "How do you know?" "I asked them, honey. Everybody is doing fine now. We just need to get you and Forrest straightened out."

"I just can't take the house from you, Mom. And you know Forrest won't agree."

Marie said sternly, "Think about the children. You all can pay what we'll call rent if that makes it better, and your Dad and me will leave that money for the other children. You might as well, honey. Nobody else wants to leave where they're at, and nobody's so greedy they want me to sell the house when they know how I feel about that."

When Sally told Forrest that evening, he shook his head disconsolately and said no. But after dinner and an hour's thinking out by the garden, he came in and said, "I'm at my wit's end, lady. We don't have enough money for next month's rent, and the kids are always a little hungry. So are we." His eyes shone a little. "There's that auto parts factory in Latchett and an air conditioning plant not far out of town. Maybe I can get a job. As long as your parents let us pay for living there, I think it's a great gift they're giving you, Sally. How good your folks are," he added in a rush of gratitude. They knew that Marie and Scott Senior would refuse to accept money until Forrest found a job. "And we'll just have to live with that," Forrest said grimly. "I'll be able to get enough repair work to keep food on the table, but there won't be money to pay them until I get a regular job." She knew his unspoken thought was, "*If* I get a job." She thought that maybe she'd look for work as well. The idea excited and scared her.

Forrest borrowed a pickup truck from the farmer, leaving the jalopy behind until he returned the truck, and they piled most of what they needed (there were kitchen appliances and bedsteads and chests and a sofa in the Ohio house, furniture that had belonged to Uncle Ray) plus Nicole, Anson, and Scott into the back. They picked a sunny day with no known chance of rain, and six hours later, they were in Latchett, tired and smothered by the closed air of the house into which they were moving. They opened all the windows, moved everything indoors, put bedding on the bed, got bologna and bread and milk from the supermarket three blocks over, ate, and collapsed. Sally was too tired to think about burning bridges behind them or about the ghosts of time past. During the night, pure cool air poured through the open September windows, and in the morning, they were refreshed and hopeful. Forrest, Anson, and Scott returned to West Virginia for the final load. Nicole and her mother began scouring and lugging furniture. It was a roomy old house, and had it not been for Uncle Ray's largesse (including some built-in bookshelves in the living room that had Nicole's full approval), their meager belongings would have been swallowed up in its relative immensity. She found Nicole crying in her new bedroom. "I don't have any clothes for school," her daughter sobbed from behind her untrimmed mane of chestnut hair and then threw her arms around her mother. "I'm sorry, Mom." Sally patted her daughter's back, crooning, "It'll be better now. You'll see," hiding her own fear.

But things *were* better. The auto parts plant was hiring. True, Nicole still had to agonize over several months of mended clothes until they caught up with things, and Anson and Scott got into a scuffle with some boys who called them hillbillies, jeering at their worn clothes, too short in arm and leg. Nicole's voice began to change as she adapted her accent to Latchett's, but Anson and Scott kept their Appalachian twang with its soft overtones.

Sally broached the subject of working to Forrest. He said awkwardly, looking off into space in the way that he had, "Well, you go ahead if you want to, but it's sure sweet to come home to a neat house and a good supper." He was working overtime at the plant and came home exhausted. Sally reluctantly put aside the idea of a job until one day Mrs. Gorman from down the street (she had brought over a tuna casserole the day after their arrival), asked her if she'd be interested in working part-time in her clothing shop. "I need to go to physical therapy in the mornings for a while," Mrs. Gorman said, pushing at her salt-and-pepper hair. "My arthritis is getting me down. I've been working hard for twenty years at that shop, and I don't think I want to come in again in the mornings ever." Mrs. Gorman's husband had been a radiology technician at the hospital, and she saw it as ironic that he had died of colon cancer. On Broad Street, only Forrest worked in a plant. Sally told him of Mrs. Gorman's offer that evening. "If you don't want me to, I won't do it," she said, out of habit and out of a feeling for the grace of husband and family that had been vouch-safed her. He answered, "I'm just afraid you'll be too tired, but if you really want to do it, why go ahead. You can always quit." And for the first time in her life, Sally had a wage-paying job. Although she did not know it at first, she was lucky that Mrs. Gorman made it known that Sally belonged to the Church family. Few shoppers treated her like hired help but were courteous and eager to make her acquaintance. Her own second and third cousins came to shop and remained to chat for a while, which, since sales went up, was okay with Mrs. Gorman. For the first time since the family had left Kentucky, Sally was surrounded by people. Her children did well in school, and Nicole got a scholarship to Oberlin, a prestigious school. Sally grew a little plump and self-assured.

By the time Nicole finished high school, Forrest had moved from the auto parts factory to Dr. Pruitt's farm. He had gone to visit the doctor several times for a skin ailment, and they had enthusiastically discussed farming. One spring day the doctor said, "Well, Forrest, I've followed most of your suggestions, and they've worked out well for my farms. How would you like a trial run as the manager of my Circle farm over on Battle Road? I can't pay you as much as the plant does, but the pay isn't bad, and there's benefits if you get past the trial months. Trial to last this summer and fall." Forrest had come home afraid, she knew, that she would balk at the idea of turning down a sure thing for a dream. But she had seen him grow slightly more bent and unhappy. He hated the assembly line. "I think you should do it," she said.

She had kept her job at the dress shop. Aretha Gorman, who had no children, became her closest friend in Latchett. Sometimes the press of cousins and other relatives grew too much for one of them, who would seek refuge in a pro-longed lunch and conversation with the other. But Aretha could not pay her very much, and during Forrest's trial period and for a year or two afterward, she would feel a cold squeeze around her heart when she looked at the bank account numbers.

He would come home, late usually, with grubby clothes and an intent look on his face, his mind still on the job. It seemed to Sally that he grew less bent, and she felt she had forgotten what a fine figure of a man her husband was, automatically using these romantic words about his appearance that she had whispered to herself when they were young. His hair was liberally laced with gray now, but it was still thick and silky beneath her fingers, and his hazel eyes seemed to gain something in luminosity as the years passed. Anson, who had the lean look of a Mercer and her gray eyes, was yet more his father's son than Scott, who looked like Forrest. Anson would go with Forrest to the farm on summer days. He was active in 4-H, which Scott treated scornfully, and after high school, he chose not to go to the community college but to work in the air conditioning factory until he was able to put a down payment on a farm of his own.

Scott grew quieter and quieter at home, though Nicole said he talked enough with his friends. He caused no problems now, though his parents were hurt by his consistent courtesy and his distance. He and Nicole were sometimes buddies, and she seemed to be in on most of his secrets, whatever they were. Finally, in response to Sally's tentative questioning, she said, "You and Dad have got to give Scott space. Believe me, he's doing okay." Certainly, he had surprised them by becoming an A student, and he did go to the community college, where he took up computer programming, transferring to Ohio State after his sophomore year. But Sally grieved, remembering the talkative little big-eared, floppy-haired boy who would come running to her with open arms it seemed not so long ago. She knew that in some essential sense they had lost him, and she had to make herself content with the knowledge that he seemed to be coping with life successfully. One weekend evening, when she and Forrest had passed him on the street, he was with a girl, a pretty girl with long dangling earrings and a narrow face. He was talking to her animatedly. Sally wondered forlornly what the girl's name was.

Nicole was already at Oberlin, majoring in English, growing ever more restless. She told her mother that she was dating, but she was critical of the young men she knew, calling them "provincial." Sally wondered where she got that word from. Finally, in her senior year, Nicole wrote to companies in New York and, with the help of one of her professors, landed a secretarial job at a small advertising agency in the Village. Only then, after she had composed her letter of acceptance, did she tell her parents. They were frantic. She was so young. What did she know about a place like New York City? But Nicole was adamant. She said her friend Winnie lived in Manhattan and would show her the ropes. They had never met Winnie. Sally thought of the years in West Virginia when Nicole had tagged along after Angela. She thought about the romantic novels set in places like New York and London that she and her daughter had gotten from the library and shared. It had never occurred to her that her daughter would take them seriously. It showed, she was sure, some unhappiness in Nicole that she had been unable to address. Now Nicole had a boyfriend in New York, and she was reluctant to talk about him. Sally thought her daughter showed strain when she talked about her life in the City, although she said that the job was great and she indicated that she was happy about the young man. Her mother thought that she was becoming secretive, like her brother Scott.

Nonetheless, the children were healthy and full of life. Anson's wife was pregnant now, and Sally looked forward, a little fearfully, to being a grandmother. She was comfortable in the dress shop, having made closer acquaintance with several of her customers, with whom she swapped stories about offspring, hers measuring up well in the scheme of things, she felt; and Forrest in trading his factory job for the managership of a large farm had become quite respectable in Latchett terms. It was not, she argued with herself, that she needed her family to be so respectable, but it didn't hurt, and if sometimes she remembered the poetry of their earlier days poignantly, she put it back under wraps regretfully but firmly.

And she loved having kin in Latchett. Cousin Millie, tall and thin and yet bouncy, her gray bob dancing in the air, would drop by and gossip about the rest of the family, mostly in a goodhearted way but sometimes with a hidden sting so that Sally privately called her Scorpio. Millie's husband owned two gas stations, and her one son was practicing to inherit them. "He's a good mechanic," Millie would say with pride and add, "so when he becomes the owner, he'll know what's what." Cousin Alastair next door was at home in the Latchett world. In the morning, as he left for the office, he would nod at her if she was out in the yard and say something like "Fine day, isn't it?" even if there was an approaching thunderstorm. He was getting secretive, dropping acquaintances right and left, and lately he never invited anyone in the family to visit him, although Millie would invade his precincts and reported that he still kept the place nice and clean.

Aunt Beatrice and Uncle Orrin, who were both arthritic and economical with movement, rarely left their farm for any reason except supplies and doctor visits, but they would invite Millie and Alastair and cousin Frank's family and Sally's family to a family picnic on a sunny summer day and again on the day after Christmas to a lavish dinner, which Sally almost dreaded because there was so much washing up to do (no dishwasher). Uncle Orrin always wore a suit that was thirty years out of date at the Christmas celebration. The rest of the year you found his stork-like figure in overalls and a plaid shirt. Aunt Beatrice wore cotton dresses year-round. She made them herself to fit her dumpy, agreeable frame, and they were always some shade of blue to match her startling sapphire eyes. Uncle Orrin was older than Marie, Sally's mother, and often spoke of her as though she were a little girl. Sally, who was amused, savored these moments to report to her mother. She and Forrest were grateful to Orrin for helping Anson negotiate for his little farm, which neighbored the one belonging to Orrin and Beatrice.

Sally felt that she had a good life, and she did not want to move to Licking County. But she looked at her husband and saw the hurt he was suffering and the damage his unhappiness was doing to them both. He was abrupt with her as he had never been and refused to meet her eyes when he came in from walking purposelessly around town. For the first time in their marriage, they were not talking to each other after they went to bed. If she tried to talk, he would grunt and pretend to be asleep. Finally, one day she said in desperation, "Forrest, do you want to take Dr. Pruitt up on his offer?"

"What offer?" he grunted and then did look at her. "You mean that about the produce market? Is that what's been bothering you? It wouldn't work, Sally. I'm pretty sure it would be closed down during the winter months. I thought about it, but it won't work. Anyhow, I knew how you'd feel about leaving Latchett."

Sally felt an enormous sense of relief, and at the same time, anguish for her husband, who had loved his work managing the farm. She thought about how he must feel cooped up in town—no garden, even—not that he had spent his days there until recently, a man who had always delighted in the countryside.

"You remember Aretha asked me back during the winter if I wanted to work full-time," she said tentatively. "She still wants to spend time writing on that cookbook, plus her arthritis isn't getting any better. I told her today I might be interested." She saw her husband flinch and thought about how he'd always taken care of them without complaining. She thought of the earthly paradise he had created on their five rented acres in West Virginia rather than complain about his work in the mine.

Now he said, turning his back so she couldn't see his face, "Well, maybe you'd better take her up on it."

So she began to work full-time. Many of the customers did not treat her with the grace they had assumed when she seemed to be doing the work as a whim. She would get tired soon after the noon hour and pray for closing time. When she came home, Forrest would usually not be there. There was supper to be got, and often she had not had time to make the bed in the morning. Forrest did nothing. If he was home, he would be sitting in the backyard if the weather permitted, staring into space. Her pay increased, but Aretha could not afford to pay for health insurance, so they were going without it. Sally prayed that nothing drastic happened to either of them.

Then one day everything changed, just like that. She came home to find the bed made, the place vacuumed and tidied, and a supper of baked beans and wieners on the table. Forrest greeted her with a tentative smile, his hazel eyes shining with what looked to her like unshed tears. "What's wrong?" she said. He tried to joke about it. "Here I straighten up and get things in shape and make supper and she asks me what's wrong?"

Happy that his bad mood had broken, she said, "Okay. What's right? Did Anson win the prize at the pumpkin festival? Or maybe Nicole got that new job?" But she was sure that the change in her husband was an internal one, having to do with his life, their life, and she repeated anxiously, "What's right, Forrest?"

"The factory hired me back," he said with a kind of false enthusiasm. "Ten years and they remember that I was one of their best workers." Without thinking, she said, "That's not right, Forrest. That's all wrong. You hated working there."

He did not deny this fact but said, with his hands on her shoulders, "But we can put good food on the table again. See what I've fixed? Steak and green beans and potatoes and I bought cheesecake for dessert. How long since we had steak? How long since we had a good dessert?" And then, more seriously, "How long since we've had health insurance?" And she was proud of him, standing there, playing the role he played so well, but she did not want him to do it. In the meantime, she said, "Well, let's sit down and have this good-looking steak. What did you put in these green beans?" But the food stuck in her throat. She visualized how her husband's shoulders would bend over again, and his cough grow racking. They were in their fifties. Would he still be around ten years from now? As they ate the almond cheesecake that she liked so much, he said, "And I don't like you working full time in that dress shop, coming home all worn out."

"If you can work in the factory, I can do that, which is a lot easier."

"I don't want you to. I want you here making supper and seeing me off in the morning," he said urgently. And she said she would go back to working part-time, hoping that Aretha would agree to it. He left the dishes for her to do, and she thought how comfortable she was with this role and how she could take that literature course at the community college, the one Nicole had suggested.

After dinner, they sat on the patio in the fragile air. He stirred beside her. "Anson called while you were at work," he said. "He says he could use some help on the farm. I can do that on Saturdays if you'll do the grocery shopping." She did not tell him that she had urged this course on her son, nor that he had been reluctant. "Won't that be too much now?" she started to ask and then thought of the edge of pleasure she had heard in his voice and said, "Yes. That's great."

That night, wide awake, Sally Anslip thought of many things, but mainly she thought, feeling the relaxed body of her husband next to her, that the poetry in her life had returned. Poetry cost a lot, of course, but it quickened your breathing and made life precious.

Mortlake Terrace

E xcept for its trees, Mortlake Terrace was in shadow. It was the early morning scene. Bronze mass of land and house, and the pale river, the paler sky. The human figures were there simply because they complemented the house. What was immediate was the rising of the sun in the row of trees along the promenade, along the river, and even that would soon enough be ember. What would arise from those ashes would be simply another such morning, and that would be sufficient. The sun would glide minute by minute, hour by hour, over the mansion's mellow stone, over the greensward, until again the landscape became a bronze shadow and human figures, returning from their daily preoccupations, would resume their destiny as protégés of the house. One of them, walking along the promenade, along the river, would stare upward into the golden nest and, belonging to the house, would feel like a fledgling returned from some tiresome, necessary journey.

Alison McCawley turned away from Turner's painting. Retrieving her belongings from the checkroom, she stared out the window into the Frick's small courtyard. The yellow tulips there were lovelier than their regimented cousins on Park Avenue. Years ago, when Alison had entered the Frick for the first time, she had done so to escape a heat wave, having meandered downtown from her steamy dump on the edge of Spanish Harlem. She had moved north from the Village after arguing with her lover about the stash of cocaine he kept in his fourth-floor walkup. Further stricken by Rembrandt's melancholy eyes, she had cried her sweaty way past the magnificent Turners in the big room and discovered the Frick version of the painter's *Mortlake Terrace*.

Now, twenty years later, she hurried to the train station. Yesterday she had told her old friend Charles that she could not accept his invitation to spend the weekend with him and his new wife. "I'm meeting Jackson upstate, just for a visit." She had a potent afterthought, somehow connected: "Charley, my brother just called to tell me he wants to sell the farm."

There was generous memory in Charley's parting words: "Be careful what you decide." She wondered if he was referring to Jackson or to the farm.

Alison had come into the city in a hurry, having left Tennessee in a hurry. She was a short woman, now somewhat overweight, and below her large, myopic eyes, her chin was beginning to sag a little, perhaps in part because she had spent years in armchairs and beds peering chin-down into books. A decade ago, she had quit a comfortable job in New York and flown backward to Tennessee. Soon her few East Coast acquaintances had forgotten to answer her letters. Her life became a round of tending house, weeding the garden, playing music to fill up the silence. Winters, when the copperheads were at bay, she took long walks in the woods and learned again to name the trees. These she said over and over to herself in a kind of litany, touching their trunks as she chanted. Finally, she was devoured by silence. She told her brother she would probably be back soon. He looked at her with the prideful loneliness that dominated her own eyes and said, "Well, all right then."

She went to visit an old college friend in Nashville and got a typing job at her old university, where she plunged via night courses, indiscriminately and compulsively, back into the organized world of the intellect. To avoid the silence, she also found a laughing carpenter who had scholarly aspirations and a wife. For four years, she circumnavigated his orbit, avoiding all risky tangents.

Finally, with the despair that attends spiritual cowardice, she wrote to her old friend Charley and asked him if his advertising firm could use another body. When, to her surprise, he replied two months later offering a training position, she told the carpenter goodbye and took a Greyhound to New York. It had been difficult getting her three pieces of luggage and her trunk from house to taxi, from taxi to station. A motley assortment, they contained all her worldly goods except most of her books, which remained on the farm. There were her few, out-of-date clothes, a gray porcelain lamp that she had found at a farm auction, a cut-glass plate that had belonged to her mother, and assorted paintings primary of hue and bold of line. These last had belonged to her Aunt Jennifer. So had half of Alison's books. (Jennifer left the family Bible to Walter because he was trustworthy and because he was in one place and because after his childless wife had left him, he had stayed on the property and kept it well. In the Bible were the names of the silent ones, absent by reason of death, estrangement, or distance.)

Lake Minnehaha (as Jackson had called it on the phone yesterday) was deep in the Adirondacks, mountain bound and green. Whitely gleaming above it was a gigantic wooden chateau that had been built in the last century for a more exclusive trade. Now it exuded a faint smell of decaying wood, and its polished floors shuddered under the inconstant feet of middle-class families spending a weekend in the country. When Alison arrived, a henna-headed woman wearing a gauzy red top and jeans was playing an ancient piano in the grand drawing room. It was out of tune. Youngsters were busy at hide-and-seek among faded brocade couches.

Alison's room on the second floor was on the lake side. The bellhop cautioned her about letting anyone join her on the sagging balcony. Besides the hard, narrow bed and an armchair with broken springs, the room contained an exquisite rosewood escritoire. Standing on the balcony, Alison was struck by a passion for loneliness, a desire to drift ghostlike among the chateau's inhabitants, out into the mountains, down into the lake. Walter would not expect her answer about the farm right away. She had always assumed that her brother was unalterably attached to the place, that he had donned his fate as unprotestingly as he had followed their aunt's commands and taken on farm work evenings after school. By Monday, yes, she must at least let him know she was thinking about buying it.

Now, though, she forgot her brother, oppressed instead by the thought of Jackson's impending arrival. Charley had taken her to lunch on her first day of work and told her he had heard from Jackson, who was asking about her. Charley had given her a five-year-old telephone number. That same humid New York afternoon, she had called Jackson, wondering if some woman would answer the phone. But it was her former lover's voice. It sounded as if he were underwater. "I do want to see you," he had said, "but not here. It wouldn't be good here. Look, remember that place in the Adirondacks." She agreed to meet him there, where they had spent their version of a honeymoon. Her fears about what she thought he would probably expect gave way to her need to pinpoint him on the map of her existence. Vaguely she thought that if need be, she could handle Jackson. Perhaps he did have someone living with him, and if so, she wondered, how would he explain a weekend away? But Jackson was a good liar.

She should have called him and put off their meeting, taken Charley up on his invitation to dine out on Long Island on Saturday and then found a Sunday nook and done her thinking about Walter and the farm. She pictured with affection Charley's now-wrinkled, friendly face and speculated about his new wife. In the photograph he had shown her, the new one looked a lot like the old one, nervous and blond and tart. There would have been space and good food and liquor. They would all have drunk a lot of wine, and Charley would have interrogated her about her years in the hinterland and told funny stories about the old days in the Village.

When Aunt Jennifer deeded the farm to Walter, she left the money to Alison. Alison was quite superstitious about those thousands, feeling that if she began to break off bits of her good fortune, it would soon disappear and with it her dream. It was not a terribly original dream, but she guarded it closely, her delicious secret that by the light of day might dissipate into some mere tawdry corpus that any conscientious psychiatrist would soon dismember.

The dream had been planted by Jennifer, having come upon her niece looking at a volume of French chateaux discovered in the back room that served in lieu of an attic. "That book belonged to your mother," Jennifer said. As she peered over Alison's shoulder, the faint citric scent of her perfume mingled with garden-scented air. "We stayed in a grand house once, Michael and me and your dad and mom. In the south of France. We traveled from your mother's family home down to Juan-les-Pins. You could see the Mediterranean from the stone terrace.

"One day, we went to Antibes, to the Picasso museum there. One of those places where he lived for a while and painted. There were urns of marigolds on the terrace, and the jetty looked black in the sun. His paintings were white and gray. Satyrs and women. And a boy, I remember a boy eating sea urchins. The sun was very bright."

In high school, Alison took French. In college, she majored in French. Jennifer would introduce her as "my niece, who plans on going abroad after she graduates."

One day Françoise McCawley had put her son and daughter into the garage, turned on the car's motor, and left, shutting the door behind her. When her husband came home and opened it, they were already unconscious. Edward rushed them to the hospital and hurried back to Françoise, who was sitting speechless on the bathroom floor. During the two years that their mother spent in a mental hospital, a glum housekeeper came to watch over Alison and Walter. Their father shrank into his books and ignored them. At his bidding, the housekeeper kept them close to home. They were rarely allowed to visit school friends. When she thought of those years, Alison the woman remembered weekday silence—fevered silence, contemplative silence, desolate silence, lush silence, silence. Of course, during fall and winter, there had been school, but they were not given a chance to play with other kids after school, and soon they no longer had any friends. On Monday through Friday, silence became second nature to the girl and boy. Forbidden expression by a puritanical housekeeper and by their father, who did not want to be reminded of them, they learned to communicate by eye and gesture. The minutest movements engaged their starved attention so that they became almost paranoiac in their reaction to unspoken nuance. Then, on Friday afternoons, Jennifer, their father's sister, would appear, laughing and kind, to take them off to the latest movie or to a new restaurant or to a children's play downtown. She became their antidote to silence. She was a tall, auburn-haired woman with light blue eyes and occasional defiance in her laughter. On those Sunday afternoons when a fellow faculty member sat with their father in the McCawley library, Jennifer might say to Alison and Walter something like: "Let's go play while the honorables are in there soaking themselves in gin and ink and generally conspiring against humankind." She spoke as though the three of them were engaged in some other, more delightful conspiracy.

The woman who had returned home from the mental hospital was not the mother they remembered, but a pale white silence who avoided their father and occasionally rushed up to hug her children as though they were in great danger. Only Jennifer could coax words from her. The veranda sun rippled on white flowers and the warm wooden floor and her long black hair as she clutched Jennifer's hand and talked, littering her sentences with French. One day Françoise sat at the dining room table and cut off her long black hair. Another day Alison came upon her in the bedroom cutting off her pubic hairs one by one. Not long afterward, Edward McCawley told his children that he was returning their mother to the hospital. *Did my mother's hands reach over and turn the wheel? The car tumbling down the mountain, the car exploding in flame. Their voices exploding out of silence.*

As Alison grew older, she asked her aunt what it was that Françoise had talked about those weekends on the veranda. "She rambled a lot, my dear. Things about her own mother, who must have been very strict, and her father, who left them when she was small. There was a garden, I think. Her mother loved the garden, and so did your mother." Alison, in search of French novels, found Colette's *My Mother's House,* and its garden came to seem to her to be like the one that had belonged to her own mother, Colette's voice to somehow enfranchise the girl's memory, give it life and grace. When Alison told Jennifer that she wanted to go to France, her aunt's eyes showed approval and excitement, but she said, "You're too young, dear, and I can't leave the farm. Wait a while. We'll go, we'll go, and Walter too."

Walter had stayed on the farm when Alison went to Vanderbilt, where her father and his parents had gone before her. She led a reticent college life, silent in a noisy crowd, reading her novels and dreaming dreams and on the weekends going home to the farm and talking to Aunt Jennifer, who was proud of her grades, proud of her dreams, dismissive of the mere children with whom Alison assured her she was associating. They went to movies together, made elaborate French dinners together, teased Walter about his silence, and wrote letters to Uncle Joe and Aunt Carla, who were living in California. Alison had never met them. "You're going to have a fantastic future," Jennifer would say every time she looked at Alison's grade report.

Alison was in her senior year at Vanderbilt when Jennifer developed cancer of the larynx. Walter took on the farm. It was not a very large farm, having in all about eighty acres—some rolling woodland, pasture given over to a few Herefords and a white Charolais bull, more acres for corn and soybeans, the white two-story farmhouse, the red silver-roofed barns and minuscule dairy, the potato field, the vegetable garden, and the large shady yard that erupted here and there with tulips, lilacs, irises, forsythia, azalea, impatiens, pansies, and the sweet williams and four o'clocks that their paternal great-great-grandmother had brought with her from Scotland.

Walter came up for her graduation and drove her home. He had himself replaced the farm manager, and he was engaged to the daughter of old Nashville friends of Jennifer. The wedding was set for late June. Aunt Jennifer was in remission, but she could not talk. She and Alison wrote notes to each other. Silences loomed. The farm became to Alison an urn of memories. Sitting in spring corners, her vision feathered by green leaves and yellow petals and blue skies, Alison thought that someday she would go to the south of France and buy a cottage near the sea, a cottage with a garden. She felt, though, that somehow she could not do this right away. She had to repair herself, her awkward, unsure, opinionated self; then she would go and live an idyllic life, perhaps with a man whom she would have found on her quest. She would seek out her mother's French childhood, and she would write there and perhaps raise a child whom she would name Françoise or perhaps Jennifer.

Walter's wife left him. Aunt Jennifer died. Fleeing silence, Alison went to New York. She planned to stay only a short while, to use the city as a point of departure. But her naive midland soul, made awkward by these possibilities that had seemed so easy in books, was arrested by the bright, crowded stage that replaced her solitary sojourn under the shadow of her aunt. As she began to move on that stage, however, and to imitate its sophisticated rhythms, she held ever more firmly to her idea of living in France. It was an impromptu definition of self that sustained her through many rude awakenings. It was an undeclared definition that froze spontaneity.

She took a job working behind the counter at an airline, and she found a small apartment in the West Village. At the airport, she was polite, rarely joining her co-workers when they made for a bar after work. Yet she was attracted by their internationalism, by what seemed to be their easy relationships, and by their easy vulgarity. They reminded her of traveling theatrical troupes during the Renaissance. Their luggage was light, their sense of fun alternately defiant and wry.

Next door to her in the Village lived an operatic singer who sang in church on Sunday and scrabbled about for singing engagements during the week. One day when they met in the hall, Alison told her neighbor how much she admired that silvery soprano voice. They began to accompany each other to hear jazz or to have a glass of wine at the bistro around the corner. They talked about men. The singer had an old boyfriend back in Scranton; Alison had no one. She was intensely dissatisfied. The stage was bright, and she had no part to play.

One fevered evening she went across to ask her

neighbor if she wanted to have dinner at the bistro, but no one answered the door. Alison spent an hour in her apartment staring out the window. Down the street was a bar she had never been in. Her singer-friend had said its floor was littered with peanut shells and men tried to pick you up there. Alison put on a red blouse and headed for it. On her third visit, she met Jackson, who painted on cardboard and plaster.

Tall and very thin, Jackson exhibited an air of moody tension that shivered in his thick mop of black hair and his concentrated brown eyes. Having moved to the Village from Kansas about a year ago, he had quickly encountered an older woman who invited him to stay with her, introduced him to marijuana and cocaine, and then threw him out when her husband returned from wherever he had gone. Jackson and Alison landed up living together for about a year, Alison's timid approach to love and sex wildly at variance with his drug-fueled interrogations.

It was time for Jackson's arrival at Lake Minnehaha. Sighing, curious, stirred, Alison went downstairs and out the door to the limousine stop. The long car pulled in dustily, and several people got out. A cracked voice said, "Alison." She hardly recognized him. He was slightly bent down, and his face had a yellowish tinge, as though he had gone to a jungle somewhere and contracted malaria. He put his arm around her. "It's good to see you," he said. His voice had lost its resonance and shivered a little. She moved automatically beyond his reach and said inanely, "Hello. You're looking well."

"You don't lie any better than you used to."

"Here, let me take the small case. Is your luggage in back?"

"This is my luggage. Traveling light." As they moved indoors, he looked around nervously. "First time I've been out of the city in six months," he said. "Separate rooms? You haven't changed a bit, Alison." He checked out his bathroom and stepped gingerly onto his balcony.

In spite of herself, she asked disapprovingly, "Are you still taking drugs?"

He shrugged. "A little of this. A little of that. Nothing to shock your pantyhose off." His dark eyes were dull and slightly glazed.

He talked all through dinner, about how no one in Soho had appreciated his work, about his long, tangled relationship with a drug addict. Someone was playing show tunes on the piano in the drawing room rather badly. He reached his hand out and put it on her arm. She moved her arm away, and without speaking, he got up and left. Alison spent the evening in a kind of bewildered distress, trying to concentrate on reading a popular novel that she had picked up in the train station.

On Sunday morning, she timidly knocked on his door. He wasn't there. After breakfast, she went walking along the high path over the cliffs. The lake was visible far below, an opaque swath on which light broke and sped. Turning a bend, she saw a man sitting on one of the wooden benches which the establishment had set up for tiring walkers. Legs sprawling, hands in sweater pockets, he was staring down at the lake. It was Jackson. She stood above him and followed his gaze. Tiny bright people caroused in a silent world. Shorn of speech and feature, they were color and form, shaped by the larger pattern of the landscape.

He turned.

"I'm sorry. I didn't mean to startle you."

He said laconically, "That's all right," and turned back around. Alison started to walk on, but he called after her, "I'm getting tired of my own company." A gentle half-smile pinched his thin, yellowed face. She came back and sat down.

To break the silence, she said, "My brother Walter wants to sell the farm."

"That place you always talked about? I used to envy you. My own problem is simpler but more drastic," he told her. "She died last month. Cancer of the colon. It lasted a long time." She saw that he was crying and put her hand on his shoulder. "Sorry," he said eventually. "Would you mind if I just went on sitting here by myself?" He put his head between his hands and shook it back and forth. Alison stood but hesitated. Jackson looked up at her with affection, "Don't sweat it. I'm leaving right after lunch. I see now there's nothing we can do for each other."

A vacuum seemed to suck at Alison. "Let's have lunch together then," she said, and he shook his head affirmatively. They had a peaceful luncheon by a dining room window that overlooked flowery banks, speaking of places they used to go to and people they used to know. He asked about Charley. Once she mentioned his partner's death, but he held up a restraining hand. Over coffee, they talked about the chateau and the lake.

"She was the one who renamed it Lake Minnehaha," he said as he got to his feet. "Got to go. That's the limo that's taking me to the bus station." He kissed her cheek. "Call me one of these days." He was gone then.

She sat another half-hour at the table, made melancholy that something so tangible as their brief life together had been should have faded to an unimportant shadow. She donned her bathing suit and went down, down the white steps to the waterside, where slowly, very slowly she entered the cold green water. She was struck by the red and orange colors of a child's swimsuit as it sat on the pier clutching at its mother's blue skirt. The father was wearing a thin yellow shirt and had his arm around the woman's waist, his hand on his son's head. Then she went plunging down, down into the icy water, and their colors seemed to rush away from her, leaving her alone, in dark shade, in her own shadow.

Leaving the lake, she walked up the hill until she found an isolated spot far above the water, and she sat there for hours. It was the first time since her aunt's death that she had spent an afternoon without her brother, without a friend, without music, without a book, without a film, without a fantasy. She thought about Jackson with surprised and melancholy respect. He had allowed himself to be touched on that quick from which people created their lives. She thought about her brother, who had visited Uncle Joe and Aunt Carla in California once and come back praising its splendors, volubly for him. Now he meant to live there. She thought of Jennifer, who had loved her, and of her parents, who must forever remain a mystery. She thought with shattering clarity that she herself had become a miser of life, had hoarded and skimped and settled for shadows. Tomorrow, she would tell Charley that she would stay with his firm until he found someone to replace her, and she would thank him deeply as he deserved. Tomorrow, she would call Walter and tell him she wanted the farm. She would build a school there fit for the progenies of Aunt Jennifers. As a talisman, she would frame her good print of *Mortlake Terrace* and hang it above her desk.

A Subversive

H er daughter went out the door, tilting a shoulder in dismissal, moving fast toward where the young man was waiting. He took her hand, and they went to join Haskell, who was fiddling with the tiller. The three of them stood there talking. Probably about the good old days in the mines, Matilda thought sarcastically.

She sat down at the table and went through the photographs that they had been putting in order. She stared at the picture of her daughter's high school graduation class. Finally, she found Naomi in the middle row, third from left. Her thumb caressed the anonymous face.

At dinner, the young man had made a fuss about her chocolate cake. "Glad you like it," was all she had been able to say coldly. He sat there young and pain-free, praising her cake and making eyes at her daughter. There was no guilt in his eyes, which were younger than the eyes of Shady

Creek men his age. But then, by the time Shady Creek men were twenty-four, they'd been out earning a living for years and had families to support. He was from Lexington, a graduate student now at Ohio State, and his father owned mines, one near Shady Creek.

Would her daughter still call the people out there bourgeois with that hint of scorn in her voice? She doubted it. The bourgeois had stolen all her children now. Her son had gone to the community college and afterward to work for a bank in Cincinnati. Her other daughter had gone to stay with him and his wife until she got a secretarial job with a big law firm. Naomi, the youngest, had lived at home until she finished at the community college and then went on to Ohio State.

Last year she had said, "I don't know, Mommy. Maybe I'd be better off if I'd never left home... I'm thinking about moving back after I graduate and staying with you and Daddy for a while. Maybe I could get a job teaching at the high school. What do you think?"

Even as hope sprang, Matilda thought, home? Where was home? Shady Creek was still home to her, but Naomi barely remembered living there. Since then, they had lived in Pennsylvania and Maryland and West Virginia, and now they lived in southern Ohio. They had left Kentucky fifteen years ago, and still, Matilda thought of selling out and going home. Haskell always said, "Honey, we can't." He had a good job here, now that he had worked himself up to being foreman at the factory. He was happy with their farm—a garden, a hay-field, and a few acres of woods. They went walking in the woods. That was about all they used them for, except for picking huckleberries and gathering black walnuts and hickory nuts. Haskell couldn't stand hunting anymore. "All the animals are disappearing," he said. "I don't even feel like knocking off rabbits."

Once in a while, some of their kin came up from Kentucky to visit and always said how lucky they were, Haskell having a good job and all their kids doing well and not that far away from home, and their nice place.

But the older she grew, the more Matilda missed the hills. They were like a secret place where suddenly the light would strike, and she could believe in magic again and maybe even in God.

Twice a year, she and Haskell went home to visit. It seemed that everybody was dying off. Her mother had died just last year. And Haskell's oldest sister had had a fatal heart attack. And this summer, his brother was dying of black lung. They had gone to see him in the hospital. He had a tube to his nose and another to his mouth. He had had a stroke, too, and he couldn't talk.

She refused to go to church anymore. For a while, she had just forgotten about God and whether he existed or not, about the arguments in her children's books. Now she was angry at him and frightened. "Honey, what'm I going to do with you?" Haskell asked despairingly.

"You didn't even cry and your own brother lying there," she said.

His face whitened and drooped. "I've cried out. I come to some kind of peace with myself about this dying business. Leastways, I think I did. But with you going on like this, I don't know."

"It's because I know now we've never going to do it."

"Do what?"

"Go home."

"Far as I'm concerned," he said, looking at her apologet-ically, "we are home. Are ye that unhappy here?"

"I don't know." It was a comfortable life. All her children

were near. The house felt good and familiar. But something in her was terror-stricken at the thought of not going home.

"We're close enough to visit," Haskell said. "We can go as much as you want."

"It ain't that," she said.

They had been married a long time. Matilda thought what a lucky woman she had been and that she was letting this get in the way. But it didn't help.

And now Naomi. The hills beckoned to her youngest daughter also. She always wanted to go there when she still lived at home. And when she went into the hills, she would put on plain dresses and leave off the paint. And put the drawl back in her voice, yes. Yes, when she said "ain't" now, it was on purpose.

Round and round and round I spun, daughter, the green hills following. It was Sunday afternoon, and Aunt Rachel and Uncle Percy and Lou Belle and god only knows who else was there after church meeting for Sunday dinner. I was past the age of spinning around like that, but sometimes when Lou Belle and me got together, we did silly things. Your second cousin Lou Belle died in childbirth two years after you were born. The midwife couldn't save her. She would have been maid of honor at my wedding, except that Haskell and me gave up trying to get Ma's consent and went ahead and eloped. I think Lou Belle's younger brothers and sisters were there that Sunday, but I don't remember. Probably. I know *my* brothers had gone off Saturday to spend the weekend with some boys over on Bear Creek. They were going to help rob the bees in a bee tree and bring some of the honey home, and they were going fishing. "And the good

Lord only knows what else they'll git up to," Pa said, shaking his head. "They better keep an eye on Hobie." When he was young, Hobie was always wandering off and getting lost. My youngest brother. I took care of him when Ma was sick after he was born. He was about eleven that summer. When you see Hobie, you see a strict man who never smiles at us when he comes down from Cleveland, a refrigerator repairman with cheap clothes and too big a family.

Pa was probably missing Hobie. The older boys were always up to some tarnation or other, but most of the time, Hobie stuck close by Pa, helping him do this and that and walking part of the way to the mines with him, them talking away as if they were about the same age. I went with them sometimes when Ma let me and walked back with Hobie. It always seemed funny the way Hobie went from talking about some new machine at the mine with Pa to being my youngest brother, mad because I wouldn't stop and go up the hill with him to see what that animal was who was making noise in the trees. When he was by himself, he'd go on up the hill, and he might be ten o'clock at night getting back home. Pa whipped him for it now and then, but it didn't do no good. And I think partly because Pa liked that about Hobie, the way he loved the things in the woods. Pa was that way, too. He never went hunting. Funny how the other boys, who took to hunting like ducks to water and who were always talking about going away to someplace else, are the ones who stayed. I think I know why Hobie left. Aside from making a living, I mean.

Pa worked in the mines from the time he was twelve years old. They didn't have any child labor laws worth speaking of back then, and when his own Pa died of TB, he went to work to support the family. Wasn't nobody else to do it since the rest of them were girls. I bet he was glad it was the reverse in our family—me the only girl. By the time he was sixteen, he was loading coal right alongside the men. (When I dream about him now, most of the time it's about that red-haired boy down there in the dark.) They had contests, who could fill up the most coal cars. They used shovels, you know, back then. I wonder what it felt like to him. His Pa never worked in a mine. Tilled them bottoms back at the old home place with corn and ran that little lumber mill. When he died, they found out the lumber mill'd have to go to pay off his debts.

Once Pa took me with him into the mine. "Just this one time," he said because I was begging to see. Hobie had already been in with him. "See it, then. I guarantee you won't like it." Black walls. Black water. Men's blackened faces and the pale shade of their carbide lamps as they came up from further down. Black wind and cold, blowing wet across my face. Pa's eyes looking at me out of that night. "A lot of the time," he said, "I have to crawl along because the top is so low."

The pay was dirt low then, Ma said. The mine owners lived in Pennsylvania and didn't give two hoots. Nobody wanted trouble, though, and I don't think the men would ever have listened to that union man from West Virginia if it hadn't been for the explosion the year before.

Eleven men dead. It got Aunt Hama's new husband. She was back home with her folks, and she wouldn't come to meeting any longer. She told Ma she was thinking bad things about God.

After Pa became a union organizer, we had a picture of John L. Lewis in the front room, beside the one of President Roosevelt.

I have heard the screams of women when their men were trapped in the mines. It was over in West Virginia.

They got word to me that Haskell wasn't hurt but was there helping bring out the men they could get to. I left Jim (Connie was on the way) with a neighbor and made the man who came with the news take me back with him. Thirty-three men were trapped. Women were calling their men's names. One of them sunk down on the ground and beat the dirt.

We were just sitting down to eat *in the green and silver light* when some men came by to see Pa. Ma had to put dinner back on the stove for another half hour. They didn't come into the house. Pa and Uncle Percy went with them out under the hickory tree, and they sat on the benches made from split oak trunks. *Pa's hair among the green like a red leaf of autumn.*

"What'd they come for?" I asked Ma while I spread a tablecloth over the pickles and stuff on the table to keep the flies off.

"It's that union business," Ma said. "I wish to god he'd give it up. Let somebody else do their talking. You mark my words. Somebody'll git hurt yet." Ma scolded as if it was a bad game. Something these fool men were up to. And if her eyes said even more to Aunt Rachel, I was sixteen and too busy giggling with Lou Belle to notice.

At last, the men got up and left. They were all nodding at each other.

Pa came into the house shaking his head. I heard Ma ask, "What was that all about?"

He looked around and saw Lou Belle and me in the kitchen doorway and said, hard worry in his eyes, "I'll tell you later."

(That's what I used to tell you, my daughter who is out there nodding at her daddy—I told you when you asked me that I'd talk to you about it later. When you grew up. How many times did I say that? Once, it was about your cousin Lily's bastard child. Did I ever tell you that one? Yes, sometime when we were looking at the pictures. Must have been a picture of her boy you were asking about.)

Ma took the chicken out of the skillet, heated up the grease, and stirred in the flour for gravy. The sun was shining on the hills. They put the kids at the old table on the porch, and Aunt Rachel said she'd be the one to sit with them today. The rest of us filled up the chairs around the big table in the kitchen. Pa said grace.

We sat over Sunday dinner *in the green and silver light.* Lou Belle and I were thinking boys. We had just got interested in some. Haskell was winking at me when he passed down the railroad track on his way to visit his aunt. I always looked down and then back up, and now I was giggling over the table with Lou Belle about it. Lou Belle was mimicking the way Haskell looked at me. She had her own boy all picked out, but he was away working in Ohio.

The children were misbehaving on the porch, throwing bread at each other while Aunt Rachel scolded.

Ma sat at the end of the table near the stove, where she could jump up and bring more chicken, more gravy, more biscuits, and then more banana pudding from the icebox. Pa sat at the other end laughing about the time him and his Pa scared the rest of the family half to death (all those girls!) past midnight, making believe they were ghosts. Uncle Percy and Lou Belle and me, hearing, laughed, too. The sun burned in his hair, leaving his eyes in shadow as he looked toward us.

(I sent Ma a letter from Virginia, where Haskell and me were honeymooning with some of Haskell's kin. "I want him to leave the mines, too," I wrote. But Haskell stayed in the mines ten years more. "Got to find something else to do first," he said.)

Your daddy has that burn scar across his chest and the pain in his right knee. I cried him out of the mines after that explosion.

"Lord, honey, don't cry anymore. I'm all right."

"I'm going to keep crying, Haskell, till you quit. Or I'll leave you." Don't get me wrong. It wasn't that he wanted to stay in the mines. At last, thank the Lord, his cousin got him that factory job in Pennsylvania.

There was a thunderstorm, and the front room was crowded with children and adults waiting for the lightning to die, except for Ma and Aunt Rachel and Lou Belle and me. We were in the kitchen clearing the table and doing the dishes. And some woman stood in the doorway talking to Ma and Aunt Rachel about how she'd put up a hundred quarts of green beans last summer. That's the way it always was.

The lightning struck a tree on the north ridge but nowhere close to home.

People bunched up everywhere in the living room. Kids sitting on Ma's trunk where she kept her quilts, sitting on the davenport arms, sitting on the floor, while the grownups took the seats.

And after a while, before we got the dishes done, the lightning died away, and there was only the rain falling, shifting walls of rain falling steady, wrapping us in quiet sound, across the steep hills, straight down from heaven. By the time Lou Belle and me got out on the porch, sun spattered the hickory tree again. Some of the grownups tried to play horseshoes in the wet backyard while others sat on the front porch and talked and watched the smaller children. As for the kids, they played ball, tag, rope until the sun began to creep behind Sarvis Mountain. Then the grownups said it was time to go home.

"Why don't you all just stay for supper," Ma said, knowing ahead of time everybody would have the politeness to say no.

"Just wants help with the supper dishes," Aunt Rachel said to nobody in particular. Then she hugged Ma. "Next Sunday after meeting, everybody come to my house."

They finally got all the children rounded up and with the right parents. Some went one way, then, and some went another until, except for Lou Belle, who was staying the night, nobody was left except Pa and Ma and me on the front porch. Lou Belle and me went in to play the gramophone. "Don't sit under the apple tree with anyone else but me," begged the pretty words that were a little scratched.

Pa and Ma sat on the front porch talking. Ma's voice rose, and I heard her say, "I don't want you to go. There'll be trouble."

"Sh-h-h," I said to Lou Belle and took the arm off the record.

"We got to hold this meeting *tonight*. We got to be ready for them tomorrow."

"You're the ones they're worried about," Ma said. "Why, if they got wind you're meeting tonight, it's untelling what they'd do."

"Can't be helped," Pa said. The silence struck his ears. "What're you girls up to in there," he yelled, and I saw him through the open door shushing Ma with his hand.

"Oh, we gittin' ready to go on up the hill for a while," I said, shushing Lou Belle. We put the gramophone away and got our shoes back on.

"Don't you girls go up past the pasture," Ma said. "It's gittin' dark." She got up, using her arms to shove herself out of the chair. "I'd better put supper on." Sunday supper was easy. Ma just heated up the leftovers from dinner.

In the rising dark, a whippoorwill brought its ghostly song near the house. "Whip-poor-will, whip-poor-wi-ill."

"They say that's a sign somebody in the house is going to die when it comes close like that," Lou Belle said.

I listened to the bird's song. It gave me pleasant shivers, the bird and the star-bit dark. "Just an old superstition," I said. "That one's been out there every summer I can remember. Least I guess it's the same one. Ever see a whippoorwill?"

"No."

"Me neither. Since I was little-bitty I heard them, but I never saw one."

We went off the porch, out the yard, across the railroad tracks, and up into the small pasture where the two cows and their calves grazed. A hollowed-out salt block stood on a ridge that was good for sitting on after the cows went back to the barn.

"Oh my," Lou Belle said. "That dew is thick. It's too wet to sit." So we went up further and leaned against a big old sugar maple. Down below, Pa crossed to the barn to do his milking. He was late. His head was bent.

"Hey, Pa," I shouted, but he didn't hear me.

I turned to Lou Belle. "Did you hear them?"

"Hear who what?"

"Pa's going to a union meeting tonight."

"In the *dark?*"

"Why don't we follow him?"

"How we going to do that? Your Ma'd have a fit."

"Hunht-uh. That's why I thought of it. She's going over to the Dalksons' after supper."

"What about when she comes back and we ain't here?"

"We might be back. And if we're not, we'll just tell her

we went to visit somebody."

Supper was quiet. Pa and Ma only said a word or two about how much milk Pa had got. One of the cows was showing signs of going dry.

"How come you girls are so quiet," Ma asked.

"Tired themselves out," Pa said, grinning at us. "Been into mischief all day."

"If you want to go on over to Mrs. Dalkson, Ma," I said, "Lou Belle and me'll do the dishes."

"Okay. I'll go on over and take my medicine early. That way, she won't be talking my ear off past midnight."

Pa set off down the railroad track with a lantern. We let him get a good start on us, spying on him through the front-room window. "What'll we do for light?" Lou Belle asked.

"Do without," I told her. "The moon's out. All we have to do is stay on the railroad track."

"What about when he turns off the track?"

"We'll see his light, dummy. We can take another lantern along in case we run into something."

"Like a bobcat, maybe? You sure we want to do this, Matilda?"

"Scaredy cat."

It was easy stepping from tie to tie. We had to be careful not to crunch down on the gravel because the rails carried sound. At first, we had to walk pretty fast to get to where we could see Pa's light.

He looked very small and all by himself.

"Can we use this lantern going back?" Lou Belle asked.

"Sure. We'll just see who's there and what they're up to. Then we'll sneak away and come home."

Almost every day, we went somewhere along the track—to the hayfield, to the grocery store, to go see a cousin or a friend, to go to school. The houses by the track had their lamps lit. I saw one of my cousins put a match to the wick in her kitchen. It had to be her getting ready to light it because her man was probably meeting Pa and the others. And it was. Above the lamp's chimney her face came out of the dark and hung there as she turned the wick down.

"I didn't think about that," I said to Lou Belle.

"'Bout what?"

"What if somebody else going to the meeting comes along behind us?"

"We'll hear them stepping on the gravel. They don't have to be quiet like us."

"Yeah, they do. Some of them men with guns may be on the lookout." And it was only then that I began to believe it.

"Silly. We'll see their lights."

"What lights?" I asked, stopping.

"Your Pa has a light."

"Maybe he hadn't ought to."

"Then let's go back," Lou Belle said. "Tell the truth, I don't feel right about this nohow."

I was about to say yes when I looked down the track and saw Pa. He was drawing further ahead of us, and he looked smaller than ever.

"No. I don't want to."

"Okay then. But I don't feel so good about it."

Uncle Percy let me shoot a gun once. It was a revolver. The kickback made me almost fall to the ground, and the noise was worse. "You want to try it again?" Uncle Percy asked after he looked at the soup can—we never did find where the bullet went. "Hunht-uh," I said, "no, indeedy."

We had been walking for a long time, and Pa was still on the track ahead. I thought maybe he was going to the mine itself, and I wanted to run ahead and tell him not to do that—them men would be guarding the mine. But he knew that.

His light disappeared. No sign of it. Then light spilled out of the dark. "The old station," I said aloud and started breathing again. "They're meeting at the old railroad station."

"Sh-h-h," said Lou Belle.

You remember that old railroad station, daughter. I pointed it out to you. A box with one side open and benches inside. It had a bad reputation with the churchgoers because some of the miners would get away from their wives and meet there on Saturday night to drink and play poker.

The Regular Baptist church was right across the track. (It was from them that the biggest complaints came.) "We'll go sit on the church steps," I said to Lou Belle. "Them trees'll hide us." We got off the tracks on the church side, going back behind the trees to the church steps.

"Well, we thought you was never goin' to git here," I heard a voice say.

Seated on the steps, we could see most of the inside of the station. Its light was made by several lanterns shining. "First sign of trouble, turn them off," a voice said, and it was Uncle Percy.

Their lanterns were on the floor. Thick light on the lower walls, showing patches where the paint had peeled off. Up above, men's faces floated in the shadow. They had cards spread out in front of them, and there was a jug on the floor, but nobody was drinking.

"Pretty smart of them," I whispered.

"Yeah," Lou Belle said. "Only it ain't Saturday night."

There were about twenty men crowded into that little place. I recognized six besides Uncle Percy and Pa.

Pa said something I couldn't hear.

Somebody I'd never seen before shook his head. "We're

gonna have guns because they got guns," he said. Whoever he was, he hadn't shaved for days.

"Those sons of bitches want guns, we'll give 'em guns all right."

"Amen."

"They won't run," Pa said, louder this time. "They'll bring in more. Even our kids won't be safe after a while. What's more, they'll blame it on us, and they'll git the law in here on their side. The sheriff's dying for an excuse to step in and help his nephew."

"Don't talk so loud," somebody else said.

They lowered their voices.

After the heat of the day, the night air felt almost wintry. We sat on the steps for a long time. Once in a while, we caught a word. The steps were hard and cold.

"Let's go," Lou Belle whispered.

But I was watching faces and listening to the whispers. There was a hardness in the sounds. If I hadn't known better, I'd have thought it was each other they hated.

We were still there when the shot rang from the hill behind us when Pa fell down. All the lights went out, and there was silence, then running footsteps past us and up onto the hillside, then another shot. "They're gittin' away," a voice shouted. "Hurry."

"Wish I had my dogs."

"To hell with no guns. Tomorrow we *all* got guns."

I ran toward the station.

"Come back," Lou Belle cried.

Uncle Percy was kneeling by Pa. He didn't ask what I was doing there. "Too late, little girl," he said. "he's done gone."

I put my hand down and felt my father's face. Even his red hair was swallowed by the dark.

At home, the last light would fall in shafts through mountain gaps, and dark rose up from the ground quickly. In flat Ohio, the sun went down more slowly. It lingered near the horizon, sending an even light across the treetops.

Usually, Matilda would have put the photographs away, done the noonday dishes, and gone to join the workers in the garden. Today, however, she remained inside, returning to the photographs after cleaning up, sitting there both looking and not looking. The pain of her father's death bit at her badly. It was a different pain now, mixed with a different knowledge and mingled with the death of her mother. Two more years had passed before the union succeeded at his mine. Two years, two more deaths, and unnumbered injuries and hatred and fear. Her father's murderer had never been caught.

She thought of absence. Her absent parents, her absent children. What if something should happen to Haskell? Getting up and going to the window, she watched him, grunting and sweating as he plowed the tiller through the weeds in the hard dirt. It was no longer possible to imagine that she had followed her mother's wishes and not married him. They had entered that circle which came with years closely shared, where the sharers no longer speak of love. Haskell simply was.

Watching and thinking, watching and feeling, she was tickled by Robert's desperate attempts to keep up with Naomi in the bean hoeing. Practice made perfect, she guessed. Naomi was a good half row ahead of him. The boy, for so he seemed to her, was beginning to look at home. Sweat had made his brown hair curl and plastered his blue workman's shirt to his back.

He was becoming part of a picture already. She saw that she was making a first beginning of separating him from that other world and making him part of her own. With a willing soul like his, and he was trying hard it seemed, it would work both ways, at least when he was with her family. He would have a smell of hill people, less than Naomi would have a bourgeois perfume, but he would have it because he wanted it. She gave him his credit in advance. He leaned on his hoe for a minute, exaggerating his panting, and said something with a laugh to Naomi. Her bitterness died a little. Some part of him would be theirs. Useless to blame the boy for what he'd as yet had no part in making.

The three gardeners put away the tiller and the hoes. She began the raspberry cobbler she had promised Naomi for dessert. Naomi was like a child about having her favorites when she came home.

The young man hung back and let Naomi and her father come first through the door. "We stink," Naomi said, laughing while her eyes looked anxiously into her mother's.

"Well, you barely got time to wash the sweat off," Matilda said with mock impatience.

"Yes, Mommy," Naomi said with mock obedience.

They said Haskell got first chance at the bathroom, but he insisted that they go first. "Going to sit here and watch your mother work," he said.

Matilda kneaded the biscuit dough for the cobbler and thought that next summer they would take Robert with them when they went to Shady Creek. "I'm a subversive," she said to Haskell.

Sunday Afternoons

O n Fridays after work he gets into his Ford pickup and drives from Columbus directly home. It takes five hours (soon it will be winter) to get to his farm in eastern Kentucky. The old truck grumbles at stoplights, quivering like a tired horse. Abraham stares ahead, shutting off pressing homeward crowds, monotonous stone walls. Here and there the westward sun builds airy cathedrals in office windows; young couples meet, their clothes gently shifting in the wind; a dapper old man sits grinning on a park bench.

The quick deaths as the truck goes by pain him. He looks ahead, then, until he crosses a bridge and enters a suburb. Here are trees, and through the windows he peers, feeding on domestic scenes: a man sitting in an armchair, a woman carrying a dress, a child absorbed in some private venture. His eyes strain forward.

For almost a year now, five days a week, Abraham has

lived in the tiny room. He rises at six and hurries so that he will have time to stop at the corner diner for breakfast before driving across the city to the parts factory where he works on the assembly line.

At home, he had risen with his wife at five and milked the cow, eaten a leisurely breakfast, and had his small general store open by seven. In the city he continued to wake early for a while but the hour's deserted loneliness soon defeated him. Waking there, he feels slothful, taking the hours as a symbol of unwelcome change, an omen of disuse and petrifaction. He has learned to dress quickly and shed his thoughts in the dark room, asserting his massive energy as he pulls the lopsided door shut behind him, striding downstairs into the brighter day.

On the job he places bolts and screws; his mind escapes, dreams, remembers; then he becomes aware of his hands, plucking and twisting; very soon his eyes blur. At noon he goes with the men in his section to a huge cafeteria. They shovel down the bland food and hurry outside to smoke and talk before returning to the ceaseless platform. He is not moved to make friends. His life lies behind him, familiar from childhood, gathered in a few-mile radius. When the bell sounds at 3:30, he often goes to a bar with three or four footloose men and downs a few beers with hamburgers and chili. And, sometimes, he goes with them to a room much like his own to play poker until early morning. His religion does not permit him to play games of chance, so he is always slightly reckless when he plays. What the hell, he thinks.

Last month, a man with a house in an outlying development invited him home to dinner. He sat in a shining metal kitchen, eating off a Formica top, being served by a strange woman. Afterward, alone in his room, Abraham was stunned by tears that welled up through his routine preparations for bed. The saltwater frightened him, dropping on the sink, forming remote, indifferent pools.

Now he travels the surrounding flatlands. Burnt grass, endless road, a few rusty bushes, factory, and near it a starchy bunch of houses. He turns on the radio, finding a country-music station, and Hank Williams sings about cold love in a lonely mansion. Familiar notes curve in his ear. His memories are dark and soft.

Over a rise and hills appear like smoky thoughts. Speed, and he is among them. Sun smiles in tall trees. Gnarled vines argue with the road. Squirrel flight. Half-seen flowers by a running stream. "As I sit here alone in my cabin..." He passes a giant rock: through a cleft a slender poplar is climbing out of sight, trunk drenched with light. He thumps his hand on the wheel in time to the music.

On a lazy summer night, tired but at ease, he pulls into the yard. The sun has gone down, but something mellow lingers. Tree frogs are chirruping everywhere. An owl cautiously intones. By the road, he has seen tidy rows of corn. In front of him, welcoming light obscures the windows. His wife steps onto the porch. Always, is that you, Abe? Foolish woman. In his gratitude, he rushes up onto the porch and gives her a bear hug, hiding his sweaty face beside her freshly washed neck. Inside there is fried chicken in the oven, kept warm by a low wood fire, and gravy, string beans, puffy biscuits with airy white butter, newly churned, and clover-blossom honey. Where's James Edward, he asks. Oh, she says, plucking at her dress, one of the Birney boys came up, and Eddie and him went off with the dogs. James Edward is fifteen now. His wife knows Abraham is hurt. Awkwardly she tells an affectionate story about some carpentry her son did in the kitchen for her. Abraham cannot speak his double pain.

Yet there is comfort in his bones. He washes off the grime and sits down to his supper at the huge wooden table, sates himself with the pungent grease of chicken and gravy, steals bold side glances at a conscious Eliza. Since he has been working away from home, it seems indecent. Better to marry than to burn, Paul says. From the low murmur of his mind he lowers his head, searching for the butter. She hands it to him, and he realizes her fingers, cool, softer than his, though callused. He does not like to think of the newer calluses; before, he and Eddie did all the hoeing except for the garden. Sadly, baffled, he shakes his head. You oughtn't to be hoeing all that corn.

She doesn't laugh it off. Eddie can't do it all by himself. He feels obscurely that she is judging him. She takes a butterfly grip on his arm. No use blaming yourself, Abe, it ain't no fault of yourn. Then quickly, girlishly, she gets up to surprise him with five mason jars of canned pears. The Sarretts brought over two bucketfuls yesterday. I put some out on the back porch. She goes in that direction.

Not now. If I eat any more, I won't be able to get up from the table. Something about her profile is a memory; he searches and finds her standing near him, smiling as he comes home in some forgotten triumph. Must have been not long after Eddie was born. A reflected grin stretches his lips.

She stacks the dishes, and they go to sit on the front porch. On the way, they pass the bedroom, and he sees the tub of bathwater where Eliza has performed her weekly ritual. Before going to bed Friday nights, they each grasp a handle and carry it to the ditch he has dug at the side of the yard. For her birthday, he brought home a huge jar glowing with colored beads of oil. Now her bathwater is tinged with an uneasy fragrance. There is something of decadence for him in that artificial sweetness; she has never worn make-up—the church is against it. Most of the women around now wear lipstick and powder and go to a beauty salon once every year or so. Finding their floury cheeks and greasy mouths ugly, yet he responds as though theirs were the beckoning eyes of Lilly Caltey, who, when he was sixteen, had very red lips; but now he frowns and averts his eyes.

They sit in the high-backed swing, silently, letting the night wind sift their faces, listening to an insistent bird.

Mrs. Sarrett said her daughter was going to be Eddie's teacher next year. Old Amos Dornes's dropsy is getting bad again. Billie Lou is going to have her seventh child.

His life goes on without him (the Sarretts had traded at his store almost every day, so had Amos Dornes. Billie Lou is his favorite aunt's child and Eliza's cousin, three times removed).

For ten years he ran the general store, bought by four years loading coal in the Bob Cat Mine. Between it and the farm, they had had a comfortable living, saving a little money. The Bob Cat closed down, and soon he was carrying more people on credit than he had for cash customers. He stuck it out as long as he could, then tried to get a mining job.

If they all move north to the city. He does not want to think about that. Her voice coming toward him in the dark. At first, she had wanted to know about the city, his job, the people he met. One weekend he had taken them to see his room. She had shrunk before its grimness, the neighborhood. They ate chicken a la king at a shiny restaurant and walked along the midtown streets. Eddie was enthralled, but Eliza did not look toward the windows of furniture and dresses. She asks him few questions anymore. For a long time Eddie has begged to go back with him to spend a week. In a way Abraham wants to take him, but who will help Eliza with the farm work? What might happen to his son while he is at work?

After getting the job, he had held off on some of his debts and saved enough to get a telephone wire strung out from the main road to the house for emergencies. It sat dumb for a month or two. Eliza didn't trust the machine; she said, who knew who might be listening in. Eddie likes it. And now Eliza calls her sister or his cousin. All that coming and going of voices. In the city the phone is natural; here it is an intruder that in his absence veers his life awry.

She says I think I hear Eddie. Flashlight strides along the road. James Edward's face falls under window shine, polite and self-contained. Look, Daddy, he holds up a burdened arm, I got a rabbit. Abraham hasn't gone hunting for three months. Plump-skinned rabbit bulges in the stained burlap sack. Put it in the refrigerator, Eliza tells her son, I'll make us a rabbit stew tomorrow. They look at Abraham. He exclaims falsely, haven't had me a good rabbit stew in a coon's age. Eddie laughs. What'd I say? Oh, I don't know, rabbits and coons, it just sounded funny. They stand and follow their son into the kitchen.

Saturday morning he milks the cow and, after breakfast, sets out with Eddie. Here and there, among the late corn, ousted weeds have revived with the help of sun and rain; he bends to pluck them out, Eddie standing silently alongside. There is that corner of the barn that has needed repairing for three years. He decides it must be fixed. He and his son drive into town to get the roofing and some nails. And after that, there will be something else. When morning comes, he hasn't time to go to Sunday meeting. Somebody must put up new chicken wire. Eddie has sneaked out of the house. Around the nails in his mouth, Abraham grumbles.

What's got into you, she says. That don't have to be done today. Eddie goes to school every day and works here in the evening. Besides, it's *Sunday.*

In her clean cotton dress, she returns to the serene Sunday house, to the kettles bubbling with Sunday's pot roast and rabbit stew. All the world is shimmering with quiet noises, the sky is deeply blue, the trees are green. He sweats and mutters; he hits his thumb with a hammer, throws the tool against a post, almost murdering a hen, and takes off up the hill. He cannot be still; he walks faster and faster into deeper woods, but at last he lingers, he lies down on a bed of moss and observes the sky, dabbles his fingers into the stream as though he were a child again. His body suspends itself in weightless lethargy. Fragments of another time hang beneath his eyelids. With willful pleasure he welds the pieces together to enter the landscape of his tenth year.

They were returning from the meeting house. *It was hot, the horses snorted as they climbed the hill.* Pa in rigid black behind the reins, Ma beside him in the gay print dress, the rest of them on the two back benches of the wagon in their accepted places, always the same, the eldest got first choice, so Abe sat in the middle. No company after church that day.

The girls go on into the kitchen with Ma to peel potatoes and break up beans.

Was that the day he was scared because Verne Caltey was at meeting? After Jacob and Luke finished eighth grade and quit school, his sisters had become Abe's responsibility. Verne kept pestering Ruth. Must have been a year or two later. Verne was sixteen and hefty; I went home with a swollen jaw. Pa was proud, but I was scared for the rest of the year.

The girls go on into the kitchen with Ma to peel the potatoes. Pa has changed into his overalls and sits in the yard reading Isaiah, a sad, hard look on his face. Jacob and Luke slip away and go courting or card playing. Jimmy, the baby, has gone to the kitchen with the women. Abraham fidgets. Mornings, evenings, and Saturdays, he helps milk, chop wood, hoe corn or sweet potatoes, keeps an eye on Jimmy.

Above the house, coming back with Jacob and Luke from the upper flat. The girls below weeding the garden, feeding the chickens, hanging out clothes.

Mornings, evenings, and Saturdays, he works. But it is Sunday afternoon, and, looking warily behind him, he goes off across the cow pasture, into the woods.

Not even the adult Abraham, who echoes now that joy, knows what change took place once the boy found himself alone. Alone in a grove, did that grave, impassive face, with its anxious eyes, relax into curly smiles and devouring twinkles? His happiness there among those elements that gave what they did not need and asked nothing in return except the work of his senses. His happiness may have been an act of love: his eyes caressing a hidden forest bloom, his fingers curving on mossy rock, his toes flapping water.

The man lies on his back. His lashes fringe his eyes; leaves fringe a spot of blue. They hover in the wind, and the blue contracts and dilates. A fleeting change thickens his sight. A cloud may be passing beneath the sun or a small gust of wind troubling the leaves. Something mantles his eyes and ears, labors his breath. The air is alive and alien; he is suspended in an indifferent sea. Already the danger passes; he relaxes, sucking in the sunny, pine-streaked breeze. A rare tornado had made its way into the hills when he was eighteen or so. They had been lucky; its center had sailed across the upper pasture, away from the house, killing a cow and crippling a horse. (For weeks afterward, he had come across markers of the storm—a broken tree, a piece of roofing from a distant farm, a huddled remnant of bird or squirrel.) He had been caught in the open, near the barn, and had thrown himself down on his stomach. The turbulent air had panicked on his back, flooded his nostrils, battered his innermost ears, and he had known for the first time that death too dwells in the air and is as intimate as life.

The tornado became a watershed of time, the past falling to one side, the present to the other; before and after the big storm, people still say, including Abraham, but this is the first time in decades that he has remembered the storm itself.

Yet on the map of Abraham's private history, the tornado arises abruptly to overshadow the surrounding terrain. His storm has shifted its center and does not occupy the same latitudes as the one marked in the almanac.

What year was it that he was almost caught unawares by a hungry panther, what year that he met Lilly Caltey back of the old railroad station, what year when his father died, when did he first turn a lover's eye on Eliza, what year when he first got drunk on Virgil Dornes's corn liquor and woke in the early morning hungover and full of sin?

But what year was it he had a pet coon, what summer that he made that sun-flushed trip to Georgia with his father? When were all those long Sunday afternoons that break upon his memories in aromatic tide?

To the first questions, he answers "After"; to the others, "Before." If he should find that the public date falls on the wrong side of the divide, his answer is accompanied by a subtle look of anguish about the brow.

The sun passes from its high center, and the shadows are in the east, and Abraham thinks of evening and his return journey. There creeps up under his lids the black-haired girl who waits on him at the diner. Her skin is white, her eyes resilient jet. Her lips match her red patent shoes, and there are blue lakes below her brows. He had met her welcoming sentences coldly, sitting stiffly behind the ham and eggs. One Monday, then, she peered from her perch at the cash register at a leather-jacketed boy approaching the diner. She blushed, she fiddled with her hair, and when the boy came in, she spoke in eager, fragile tones. Why, she's young, Abraham thought. Now she tells him about her boyfriend, and he complains about the weather. Friday morning, she ran after him to return some extra change he had left on the counter and watching her run toward him, heeding her friendly voice, he had thought, I wouldn't mind... I wouldn't mind if James Edward had a girl like that one.

Suddenly wary, Abraham shakes open his eyes, stands up, and sniffs the air happily. On the way home he picks goldenrod for the house and whistles. Eliza is sitting by the kitchen window; her worried face is blissful power. He goes through the door laughing and hands her the yellow scrolls. Her worry dissolves into relief and pleasure so fast he laughs still more. Eddie comes back, and they go out together to feed the hogs. The family sits down to Sunday dinner.

He eats slowly the mashed potatoes, the spicy meat, the lettuce and green onions killed with hot bacon grease. Eddie is clowning. The light from the dangling bulb expands and casts a blessing. As his stomach grows heavy, the shadow of his departure grows until there is a film across his eyes, a curtain over his ears. He eats more to sate the ghost.

Eliza says, I met Jacob in the A&P on Monday and I said he was to tell your mother we'd be up there next weekend.

Thin face, rough red braids, soft, soft eyes looking at the—what was she doing?—*by the well, bending over, pulling in a bucket of water.* That must have been when I was ten or so.

She will die soon. The last time, cheeks falling into her toothless mouth. He sees the farm, the rich soil where he and his brothers had helped their father clear new ground, the hill flats, weathered, unpainted house. I was ten.

Sunday after church, Pa's sister Claudie and her family. I went to the coalbank (cool, dark quiet, the sun outside, bright and thick. Claudie's children yelling at me) to fetch another gallon jug of milk. All that's gone now. Only a few old people. Jacob had electricity put in years ago, a refrigerator. Luke and Ruth dead. Isaac in Roanoke. Esther and her husband in Detroit...

That's right. We'll go next Sunday.

Not me, Eddie says, pushing his chair back. Abraham looks at his son, whose hands are intent on the table's edge. What do you mean, not you?

Ah, there's nobody my age up there. Just a lot of old folks, sitting and gabbing. James Edward rises and starts for the door. I'm going over to the Sarretts with Bill Birney to watch some television.

You listen to me, young man. You're going with us next Sunday if I have to drag you by the ears.

Eddie freezes. Eliza tightens her lips, gathering spoons. He shoves his chair back, steps tightly around his son, goes out, and sits down heavily in the swing. He hears his son leave by the back door. His anger ebbs, leaving fear.

157

That night in the bar with Jacob's boy. Davis had called him at around ten in the evening. Abraham was trying to read a western. Well, son-of-a-gun, he said. Good to hear a voice from down home. Frosty March poured through the open window.

The table was scarred with cigarette burns and knife gouges. Davis and his girl on the other side in dim, smoke-choked light. Howdy, Uncle Abe, the boy said, meet Hallie, she's from down our way. Pink sequins, powdered face. Light poured through the squat whisky bottles, lay trapped in amber pockets. Oomph, bang, boom went the jukebox. Davis and the girl were dancing. He was Jacob's youngest. Had a truck driving job now. Lines of laughter pinched his cheeks as he danced, a good-looking boy with fair, rumpled hair, broad cheekbones, mischievous brown eyes. Hadn't been home for six or seven months. He had quarreled with Jacob, who didn't like it because his son wouldn't haul himself out of bed and go hear his daddy preach on Sunday. (You mark my words, Jacob growled, that boy's up to no good. I don't know, Abe, what this world's coming to.)

Young. Five years after I left home before I married. Hopping the freights out to Colorado and back. Liquor, cards. Like all the rest. Women. But Davis is almost thirty. Met that girl in a bar.

His nephew had gone over to another table, and she said, Goddam Davis, treats me like dirt. He asked her why she went with the boy, then, and she answered, nobody goes with Davis, depends on what skirt he happens to remember what night. She stood by the jukebox, shoulders bent, face heavy with a vague, general sorrow. Abraham sat studying his nephew, who had wrecked three cars in two years and had spent two nights in jail for disorderly conduct. He picked a fight now with a bearded kid and

Abraham got up to stop it, but somebody else stepped in first.

Abraham had taken a bus to meet them. Lights had plucked at his thoughts, moving past, gravely beautiful, as they do weekly when he returns from home in the early morning hours. They offered some abstraction he could not grasp, a string of luminous moments joined by the moving bus, disappearing as the bus went down a dark street, shattering into static fact when it halted at Plum & Main.

Abe? Abe? You been sitting out there a long time. It's after nine. Her face through the screen door.

It's almost time to go.

The walls of night recede. Far away hangs the frosty blade of a new moon. Between heaven and earth only one secret. Fragrant rumors of thin drifting air.

It's time to go.

Eddie still gone?

Uh-huh.

Where'd him and the Birney boy go off to?

She sighs. I reckon, watching television.

He better come up and spend a week with me next month. If he still wants to.

She looks frightened.

He'll be out of high school in two years.

He gets good grades, she says defensively. God only knows what he thinks about, though. She smiles. Last I heard, he was going to be on television.

The swing creaks as he rises. Eliza comes through the door. Like a soft word, his arm goes around her waist.

I put up some ham sandwiches in case you want a bite to eat when you stop for coffee.

Too late for anything else now.

The prow of his truck shatters the night, sending wakes of air to join the rumors behind him.

He passes the old Dornes homestead. (Things are getting real bad, Jacob said. You know Al Dornes's son, the one you used to run around with. Well, he's got seven kids, and he's been out of work for more than a year. Yeah, I know. Oh, I guess we don't know the half of it, Jacob said. The Jarnises never had much, but we always had land. Leastways, we got a place to come home to.)

Yeah, for the time being. Out of the corners of his eye on the way home, thin children in ragged blue jeans, gray shacks, men sprawled on the porches, but he is always so happy to be coming home. And when he leaves Sunday, it's dark. But then they were there before. Eliza's cousins coming into the store, charging everything. And others, the ones he didn't give credit to.

Got the blues sitting with Davis in that bar. Whisky. I shouldn't have drunk it. *The room was close. It was hard to breathe.*

Things are worse now.

He passes Tom Willis's tavern. Neon lights crashing over the hillside. Willis is in on everything, buying votes, that business with the justice of the peace, brawling, whoring. But he can tell the best whoppers in three counties. It brightened the day when he came into the store. Not a mean man, no. There are others, the Caltey men, mean from the day they was born. Stop at nothing.

Davis said, Yeah, all you good churchgoing folks. Oh no, it wasn't my old man and you that used to run around with Tom Willis, oh no.

Anyhow, the Jarnises were never that kind. The boy had looked tired, glancing over at his girl. Two heavy lines plowing his cheeks. Hate in his eyes. Bad. Believing in his own sin.

Walking away from that bar in the wind. No one else on the street. Wind doesn't stir buildings, only saw it shaking my jacket. The night was cold, but whisky burned in my head. *Evil everywhere. But here, here it existed without his consent. Here life existed without him, skidding along directionless roads. He shivered and contracted, hurrying to his room.* Room 4M, 190 N. Fifteenth Street.

At midnight he parks at an all-night truck stop and orders coffee. Standing by the pickup, he opens one of the sandwiches, uncreasing the wax paper as though it were a love letter. He is not hungry, but he eats it. A light rain begins, and he lifts his face to receive it.

Back in his room, he tumbles his clothes on the floor, falls into bed, and immediately goes to sleep.

Vast highway amid trickles of light. Harsh rhythmic sound singing behind his ears, accelerating, warming up. Light rays smash his windshield and thud against his eyes. He is on foot, running on sand. The wind. The yellow sand and the red truck. No odor for the course, no color for the weight, the wind.

He wakes and listens to the rain on the roof, but the surf in his ears has a vaster sound. Sighing, he swings his heavy legs floorward, lights his three-dollar pipe, opens his book. The apes are muttering, the quiet man rides the trees, keeping his hand on his knife. The heroine runs through the vines, seeking to warn him of a yet nameless villain. Suddenly it seems to Abraham that she will be too late. He reads faster, with shallow breath.

Saved. He lets the book fall by the bedside and looks

intently, blindly at the khaki-hued spread, the wrinkled pillow, the cracked walls. Downstairs a stifled radio bleats weakly of love and sin. He turns off the light and lies very still for a long time, regarding the brick corners that intrude upon his single window, the penny patch of sky.

He must sleep, but he is afraid to dream. Now is the time for all good men to pluck gentle memories from the dark and bathe their burning eyes. There is a mild farm hundreds of miles away. Let it be noon and the acquiescent willow drape the form of his sunlit wife as she prepares warm red tomatoes for canning. Their juice turns to rabbit's blood. He groans and turns to watch his son throw out a practiced arm to catch the ball. It curves upward to shatter not Eddie's brow but the gaunt eyes of Abraham's father. Eluding panic, he opens his eyes. It is hot. A rough damp hillock of spread imprisons his feet. It is hard to breathe. He rises to sit in a chair stuffed with the ages and upholstered in mildew. He opens the small window and turns his nose upward to a frail and distant moon and shakes his head. Leaving the window open, he picks up his book and returns to the chair.

Going Home

H er grandchild has been moved into the room where its mother sleeps. Sometimes Coralee dreams that she hears the baby shriek and, wakening, she stretches out her hand to make sure her daughter still sits on the stool. "I want to go home," she whispers.

"Sssh. I told you. As soon as Delbert comes."

She hunches down in the mattress, swooning in the half-sleep of high fever. The boiler had broken down, leaving the building without heat for two weeks, and she had weathered that gray cold well, lying in bed most of the day with the baby beside her and stifling her longing for a good coal fire flaming out of a grate. Now the heat was back on, and she had a fever.

They had been strip-mining back up on Silver Knob, and Delbert came up the holler and said, "Mommy, now you got to move. That next mud slide will hit the house for sure. We got the back room ready. You come live with us." She was in the kitchen fixing new potatoes and gravy on the electric range. It sat beneath the window where the coal stove had been. Delbert and Maybeth had given it to her last year when he got so much overtime. She had watched them carry the old stove out and junk it, remembering her young husband jumping out of his uncle's truck, throwing off the tarpaulin with a flourish, revealing the coal stove, black and shiny green. He was buried on the hill above, his headstone visible from the kitchen window, above the graves of his parents, with the gap beside him where she should lie. She heard the clatter and roar of the machinery gutting the mountain as she said, "Reckon I'll stay put."

She took a notion, though, to go up to Chicago and visit Tilda Jean for a week or two. Tilda had been begging her to come. The baby was due next month. Tilda's man had taken himself off with some whore, Tilda said, who served drinks at the restaurant where Tilda waited on tables. About what you'd expect of him, the mother thought as she packed the warm quilt her own mother had made for the baby Tilda. The house full of chattering women who grouped themselves around the quilting frame suspended from the front-room ceiling while the men went to see how the catfish were biting in Sarvis Creek.

She had to go and get her daughter to come home.

Coralee had had a hard time with Tilda. Old Rachel finally stopped the bleeding and said, "We'll git you into town." The doctor performed a hysterectomy. Her man was out of work that year, and his brother paid the doctor bills. It was a long time before she got back on her feet. Her milk had dried up, and condensed milk didn't agree with Tilda. Every day she would go out and pick ground ivy to make tea for the baby's colic.

But at three, Tilda had an angel face. Until she went to that new consolidated school in the coal camps. Red lipstick and rhinestone earrings dangling from uneven, festering holes. The older men and women at meeting, the church by Sarvis Mountain where Coralee had become a bride, shook their heads and predicted a bad end. Tilda's father shook his head and said, "I done my best with Delbert. Tilda's up to you." Tilda got a job in town at the five-and-dime. It seemed to her mother that she picked the dirtiest young men in the neighborhood to walk out with, and finally, Tilda had taken up with the married man who managed the five-and-dime. They ran off to Chicago, where he had some cousins.

A year passed. The family's grief had settled down to an ache that hid itself behind their everyday lives, although the mother would wake up at night out of a dream in which her daughter was butchered or raped on some dim street.

Now she'd started a baby, and he'd run off. About what you'd expect of him. Coralee put the quilt into the cardboard box that would go with her on the bus and walked out into the yard. Her hollyhocks were blooming. She sat down beneath the oak tree around which, in the good years, they had had water fights: Delbert and his daddy on one side, her and Tilda on the other. Around and around, through the house and up on the hill, giggling and silly. He caught me after dousing me with half a bucket, his arms tight, hauling me off behind the chicken house. She looked up to where only a bleak scar remained of the limestone cliff, the pines and the oaks, the stand of black walnuts. Visiting Tilda was a good idea.

"Never bin out of the hills," she said to her son as he reluctantly drove her to the bus station.

The minute she got off the Greyhound, she wanted to go home. Tall buildings stabbed the sky, and her ears were choked with noise. It was worse uptown where Tilda lived. Somebody had messed hisself on the street outside the building. There were two bars in sight. Country banjo music came loudly out of one of them. She asked Tilda about the cousin who had come up last year looking for a job. "Couldn't find no steady work. He heard from his brother there was some in Detroit, so they moved on."

Tilda was crying in her arms, and the unborn baby moved. Oh, my honey, my child. Why'd I ever let her leave home? That ornery lowdown stinking man. Where is my baby's pretty skin? My daughter's eyes are dull and old.

They fried hamburgers on the hotplate, and she slept in the living room.

On Sunday, they went downtown to the park by the lake. Whenever Coralee turned to look at the lake, she could feel the buildings crouching at her back.

When Tilda was at work, she stayed indoors, though Tilda urged her to get out by herself, go take a look at Marshall Fields. Tilda didn't want to go home. The restaurant owner had bought her a pair of imitation emerald earrings.

When the contractions started, the man on the next floor up let Coralee use his telephone. He was chewing gum, and his ragged mustache bounced up and down.

At the hospital, they made her stay outside in the waiting room. A colored woman, sitting on the other couch, said, "It shore is hot in here." Large and comfortable looking. Large comfortable voice with a Southern accent.

"It shore is."

"Somebody of yours having a baby?"

"My daughter."

"How many's she got?"

"It's her first one," Coralee said apologetically.

"My niece, she already has four, and she's in there workin' on her fifth one," shaking her head. "I told her not to marry that no-account."

"My daughter, too," Coralee said. "He went off and left her. Just like that."

They shook their heads in unison.

Tilda looked young and rested the next morning, propped up on the pillow, combing her hair. It was a boy. Seven pounds and two ounces. The grandmother stood outside the glass window, her hands flattened on the pane. Wizened and somber, the little red face in sleep twitched fretfully. Its pied hands formed fists on the anonymous blanket. Coralee felt things she had never thought to feel again.

Some other woman was having pains, and the doctor came by, stopping beside Tilda's bed. "You're doing fine," he said jovially. Coralee offered him a chocolate from the box she had bought downstairs in the gift shop, but he flopped his hand and turned away. "See this young woman gets plenty of rest." His face was unlined, and his hair gleamed under the light.

Back in Tilda's place, Coralee found that she was jealous. She had expected to take care of the baby, but Tilda was crazy about it. The old woman watched her daughter nursing it, the soft, healthy look on the younger woman's face. Afterward, Tilda would gently lay the baby in his grandmother's arms, and she would burp him, beating vigorously on his back while his head lolled in the crook of her neck like a small bird in its nest.

When Tilda went back to the restaurant, someone else had her job. "He promised he'd save it for me," she cried. "That bitch is shacking up with him."

"You watch your mouth!" Coralee said.

How could she leave Tilda? If Tilda got a job, who'd take care of the baby?

Coralee fell into a despondent lethargy. She met somebody from down home in the supermarket where she was buying Spam and light bread. The woman came back with her to Tilda's place, and Coralee asked her new friend how long she'd been up here. "Lord, ever since my man lost his job in the mines. Must be nigh on seven years now." Now her husband was a janitor in a big apartment building downtown, she said, and they lived in the basement. "Only reason I'm uptown, I come to see my sister. She moved up here with us."

"What's your sister do?"

"Little of this and a little of that." After two more cups of coffee, she said her sister was on welfare.

"Why don't she go home, then," Coralee asked anxiously.

"Aaiih, ain't nothing for her down there. My brother now, the one that's next to me, he'd take her in. But she don't get along with his wife. Never did. Besides, who wants to go back down in there?"

"I do," Coralee said.

Sometimes a loudmouthed woman with dyed hair came to visit Tilda. Coralee would nod distantly and retire to the inner room, taking the baby with her. Through the door, she could hear the glasses clink and the way they talked about men.

She'd been up here for three months. She'd had going home in mind ever since she stepped off the bus. One Thursday, after Tilda's loudmouthed friend left, she felt desperate. Ignoring the baby, she said, "I'm going home Saturday morning. I'm going down to the bus station and get me a ticket, and I'm getting on that bus and going home."

Tilda thought her mother talked of going home because she hated Tilda's friend. "Now, Ma, she's all right. Talks too much, but she's got a good heart. Always been good to me." She patted her mother's shoulder placatingly. Coralee smelled sour whiskey. She looked inside the stout cardboard box where the fair baby lay regarding the ceiling with trusting blue eyes. "Why don't you come on home with me?"

"Ain't nothing down there for me, Mommy."

"Your home's there. Your brother Delbert, he's got a spare room."

"What would I do?"

"You could get a job in town. Maybeth and me'd look after Howard."

"I want to stay here," Tilda said. "I like living here."

"You mean you'd have to behave yourself down there. In front of your kin," Coralee snapped.

Tilda cried half the night.

Coralee didn't go.

She kept having a dream. She was walking through the woods on her way home, and she was lost. A policeman jumped out from behind a tree and said, "It's not here any-more." Around dark, there were a lot of policemen on the streets where Tilda lived.

Tilda got another job waitressing. That meant she

couldn't nurse Howard anymore, and the grandmother would feed him his bottle. His minute grasping fingers were a web wherein she would become forever bound. Now, as he snuggled his small soft self insistently against her and clutched her neck hairs as if they were the only links between him and oblivion, she was lost. Clucking her tongue, she washed his undershirts and told him about the way things used to be.

Tilda bought herself two lipsticks, one pink and the other red, and a lavender dress. Nights, when she thought Coralee and the baby were asleep, she slipped upstairs to visit the man with the phone. They turned the radio up high. The mother could hear their feet swooping on the wood floor and, later, other rhythmical sounds. Coralee was tired. Her prayers stopped at the ceiling. I reckon the Good Lord stayed behind, she thought.

Her daughter bought the baby a green romper suit with a blue car embroidered on its pocket and bought Coralee a dark cotton dress and a new pair of shoes and a steak at the restaurant with all the trimmings. She held her grandson while Tilda drank beer and gossiped with the other waitresses.

Arthritis struck her hip, and Tilda finally got her to go to the emergency room. Tilda and the baby went along. They had to wait a long time. As Coralee sat dressless and shivering on the cold metal table, through the glass wall she saw Tilda sitting in a chair surrounded by pale, unhappy strangers, clutching the child loosely, her head down like a rabbit.

Delbert wrote to say he had moved all the way over to Sarvis Creek. Silver Knob was a sight. One corner of her house had already been damaged by a mudslide last month during that big rain. The kids all missed her. They'd fix up the old smokehouse back of his house when she took a notion to come on home.

As she lay in bed with the fever, Tilda read the letter to her.

"You ain't leaving nothing out, are you?"

"Now, if I told you he was begging you to come on home and leave me here all alone with Howard, what could I be leaving out?"

Pain and misery.

> Goin' down the road feelin' bad, oh Lord.
> Goin' down the road feelin' bad.

The beast jumps off the ridge and puts its paws around her throat. She wakes up sputtering and stretches out her hand. Tilda stands over her, feeling her forehead. "Drink this water," Tilda says worriedly. "I called the nurse, and she said to give you liquids." Her daughter tenderly tugs the quilt over Coralee's shoulders.

Coralee holds her throat. "I want to go home," she mutters.

"We're going, Mommy. Soon as you get better. You and me and Howard."

Coralee grasps her daughter's hand. "Something happens to me," she says breathlessly, sitting up in bed. "you still go." Cagily, "For Howard's sake."

"Yes, Mommy."

"We can live in the smokehouse, and you git a job in town, and Maybeth will help take care of the baby."

"Yes, Mommy."

Before she slips away forever into the homeless dark, Coralee retires to her place inside the limestone cliff, where water has hollowed out an open cavern so long ago that moss covers the floor, flowers grow there, and a young sapling. All day she has mopped and churned and cooked, baked, cleaned, made up the carrot ridge. Green rustles over all of Silver Knob, and the spring wind spreads the smells of pine and honey-suckle. Her children play barefoot. He comes home from work and, stripped to the waist, is washing off the black in the basin by the well in the backyard. The chickens squawk lazily in the new heat. The cow moos in its pasturage. Tomorrow Pa and Ma and all the others, even Uncle J.B. from down in Virginia, too, are coming to Sunday dinner after church. The fryers are plucked and cleaned, ready for the stove. The ham is ready to bake. She has made a cocoa fudge cake, and two lemon meringue pies, and rice pudding. The men will go fishing at the other end of the bottom where the big cats are, and she will sit with the other women on the porch and talk. Her children will play ring round the rosy with their cousins in the front yard. Green rustles over all the mountains, and in their circle, the sun rides high.

His Story

Most deeply, in the fallow field where language drew its sustenance, she remembered her father's hands. They were broad and of medium length, with the nails lying thick and broad across them, one nail black on the squashed finger that a machine had run across in the mines. She did not know the name of the machine. They were callused hands, the skin tough, hued red and brown, and when she remembered them most poignantly, they were removing an engorged tick from a hurting dog or a "wolf" from an ulcerated cat neck or putting some kind of drops in its ears to kill the mites. Her father was often an unhappy man, and sometimes for months, he was severe and morose, but his hands tended the dog, the cat, the calf, the chicken, the pig, a squirrel.

Later, after his accident, when the disability payments came in, he would call a vet, no longer in command of his skill.

A Kentuckian from the hills, he had left home first in search of adventure in his youth, hopping the freights to Oklahoma with a friend, taking his young wife to the shipyards of Jacksonville during the big war; and then had left his youth behind, in desperate search for a job to feed his growing family. By the time his daughter had reached her thirties, she knew enough to stand in awe of his feat. Having only an eighth-grade education, he had scrabbled from job to job, taken home correspondence courses in electrical matters so that he learned to repair refrigerators and radios, and then got a mining buddy to help him qualify as a mine electrician. All the family had, of course, scrabbled from place to place as mines closed down during the bust years. And he had kept them together. Her mother had stayed at home with the seven children. He had kept his biddies as safely as he could, as safely as they would let him, as safe as God and nature and humanity would let him, far safer than it was safe for them to be, under the light while with his callused hands and his large sorrowful head he took on the vast and alien world that lay beyond his homeland.

One summer night the year before he died, he sat with her, his oldest daughter, Daisy, at the kitchen table, oak, polished by his youngest daughter in the tradition of perfectionism that he had instilled in his children, in the aesthetic and class-consciousness of the bourgeoisiedom to which he had aspired as to a safe haven, to which his children had, with his consent, defected. He sat there half-blinded, crippled by arthritis, with a corkscrew spine from the injury, drawn lower by a foot from his natural height, diabetic, dependent on the care of others, and he reminisced with a sweet, mild light in his eyes.

"We worked up on Tanker Fork that year, Otis and me,

in the lumber camp, and ever weekend we'd go on home, over to Sarvis Creek. Up Tanker Mountain and down the holler where Jarvis Bright still lived with his ma, and then along the Big Muddy Road."

He sits quietly, forgetting that his daughter is there, looking back, looking in, looking at that young self who had lost his father when he was six, his mother when he was ten, and who had started carrying pipes for a natural gas company when he was thirteen.

"It was way after dark when we got to Rusty Creek, and ever dog up and down that road was barking at us. Weren't none of them tied up. This one old big fellow, black as coal, took a bite out of Otis. I was scared."

It is an admission, an abdication of responsibility that she thinks he has never made before. She senses that he has at last given up the role that he undertook so many years ago when he married the young girl with the coronet of braids, the role to which he had been destined as his father's son, the role which ran counter to his young rebellion in the years before marriage when he was known in three Kentucky counties as Wildcat.

Photographs tumble into her mind, the photographs from the old shoebox that she has looked at with her mother in the afternoon. Young, he sports a cowboy hat, his curly hair hidden but his lean, handsome cheeks, his startling blue eyes revealed. He is smiling at the picture-taker, at his wife and daughter, who are bending over the shoebox. In another picture, he is holding her, his firstborn, on his knee, in the backyard on Sarvis Creek, beneath the Golden Delicious tree that wide-limbed grew there, in the hollyhocked yard, and in a small joyful wind, his curly black hair blows jauntily, his hands hold his three-year-old daughter carefully, while his blue eyes smile at the young mother, his young wife, who is snapping the fuzzy picture.

Wild anguish and anger rise in Daisy, even more potently than in those days after his factory accident, when, living in New York, she heard her mother's voice say, "He'll live. That's all I can say. He'll live." But it had disabled him, that splendid active man who was her father. Years of enforced idleness seemed to lay ahead, though as they had passed, he had worked in the yard and garden, fighting pain with every inch of him.

Now sitting there across from him at the oak table, she tries to remember why she had not gone home, those years when her own life had seemed so pressing and difficult, so entangled was she in her own head, trying to make her way through the labyrinth that coiled about a center where the hills seemed to stand forever near, forever unreachable, a labyrinth of sights and sounds and smells and other people's thoughts and imaginings that assaulted what Camus called "the warm innocence of poverty" and which encompassed so much, the discrete family life now fragmented, the circle of the hills breached, the childhood left abruptly behind in the hills that it too was a whole and beautiful thing, a mythic landscape whose rumor even reached the streets of Manhattan. It seemed unthinkable to her now that she had not taken the Greyhound home to see her father; that she had spent her love in apocalyptic moments and kept on going in that life which never would cohere because she had for so long not accepted that her roots were deep into the mountain soil so that the mythic tree would grow in limb and heart and mind.

The night her father died, Daisy lay in bed in the stifling dark (the radiator knob was broken, and she couldn't turn the heat down) and, as she waited for the dawn and her early flight to Ohio, relived an experience of her thirteenth year.

They had been living in a coal camp named Oretown, in one of a string of gaunt gray houses perched above a dark greasy river down whose banks the coal camp inhabitants threw their garbage so that there was always a rich stench in the wind. In front of the houses ran the railroad tracks on which the carloads heaped with coal came past from the mine where he, her daddy, worked.

Daisy had been afraid and unhappy ever since they moved to Oretown, and now in August, she longed feverishly, endlessly, for the green and gold spaces of the Kentucky hill summer to which she had been accustomed. She had taken lately to surreptitiously taking out the Bible, which her mother kept tucked away in a dresser drawer, along with the birth certificates and the loan papers. After everyone else had gone to bed, she would take it to the kitchen table and open it up, as her Bible school teacher back in Kentucky had told her people did, though he said it was superstitious, and see where it fell open.

That night the Bible had fallen open to the Gospel according to St. John.

In the beginning, was the Word, and the Word was with God, and the Word was God.

The same was in the beginning with God.

All things were made by him, and without him was not anything made that was made.

And lying in bed awake in the West Virginia dark, the girl thought about the Son of God and about God the Father, and she thought about the generations of man, and back and back in time she went. If Christ had no grandfather, then back of God she felt nothing but nothingness. She felt nothingness press, press, and expand until it took over the night and robbed the sky of the moon and stars.

The flat landscape developed bumps as they moved southward behind their father's body. When at last the hearse and their car crossed the Ohio (muddy with spring rains, flooding over its banks), there on the other side, the hills rose like a green wall deflecting her vision. Daisy asked her sisters what time it was.

She had not been to a funeral since her third year when wailing women had followed a men-borne casket up a hill flickering with redbud and dogwood, she tightly holding her mother's hand, scared by the wailing and by her mother's preoccupation. Her father had been straining forward bearing his share of the coffin, and she could not see his head. Panicked, she shouted for him, and he lifted bruised eyes (his youngest sister was in the casket) above his load and smiled at her.

(In the Ohio orchard, by the Chinese chestnut tree that he tended so constantly, because it reminded him, she knew, of the late lamented American chestnuts belonging to his Kentucky childhood on Sarvis Creek, high up where Sarvis was a hollow flowing down Sarvis Mountain, where the trees were old, old and high and broad and green, where the lumbermen had maybe never yet been, though they came later: in the orchard, by the chestnut tree and to their left the blueberry bushes, the pear trees, the apple trees, the plum trees, the peach trees, two of each, and the Jerusalem artichoke, all planted by him, and to their right the stretch of field he left fallow because on it were the wild strawberries, the raspberries, the blackberries, the dewberries, and the hickory trees, all growing wild there, as they did in his childhood, up on Sarvis Mountain: in the orchard by the chestnut tree he said to her, as she paused with the mower, "All I ever wanted for my daughters was that they grow up to be like their mother." That was all he said about her decision to return to New York. In it, she read his despair that his oldest daughter had become a stranger. She paused yet and looked at him, his painful body, his eyes turned inward on the pain, on memory's fields as well. She had longed, as she often did once past her thirtieth year, that he would descant in rich narrative all those pent-up tales, the secret of his life, so that she might recapture something she had lost. He bent his body over the cane and walked on to the hen house with the fresh straw that he had slowly, slowly gathered for the nests, and she had started up the mower and moved it in and out among the trees, feeling like a familiar dream the country sun on her scalp, her arms, her hands.)

As the car followed the hearse through the town of Ashland, Kentucky, once they were past the streets of pretty houses whose yards were green and crocus-spattered, they passed giant structures of metal emitting smoke. One structure had fire flaming from several of its chimneys, like some giant botanical creation, the sturdy stem of the pipe and then the gaudy red and orange flowers of fire, a Van Gogh eruption from the earth, as though nature and men were entwined in a conspiracy of dream, of art. She thought of her father, who had worked in such places as well as in the mines ("Miles of asbestos," he had murmured half-asleep, half-dreaming in the hospital after they gave him the asbestos tests. "Johnny and me wrapped the pipes. Miles and miles of it").

She thought of her father sitting in the backyard in Ohio, in a cane chair turned to the west and beyond him arabesques of pink and orange clouds in a deepening blue sky. Her mother had come up beside Daisy where she was watching her father through the kitchen window and said, "Back home, when the weather was good, he would always go to the old bench at the top of the hill and watch the sun set. Remember that old bench?" And Daisy did remember it, and her father sitting there, but she had not paid attention. The others were too young to remember the bench, she thought, but Alison, the second sister, lifted her voice and said, "I remember it too. I used to go sit with Daddy ..." her voice had trailed off.

They sat in breathless silence for most of the rest of the trip, except that Jessica, the youngest, who was driving, said, "I wish we'd get there," and then added quickly, "but I don't."

They reached Sarvis Mountain at the time when he would have been watching the sunset, and after the interminable business of placing the casket in the church ready for a viewing that evening, they were greeted by people they hardly knew: by the brother and sister who remained and by the nieces and nephews old enough to remember his youth and by the mining buddy he had had and by others who remembered Wildcat with fondness and amusement. Their heavy hearts both resented and accepted the amusement. It reminded Daisy more than anything else that he had been a young man once, a young man who touched others' hearts. She saw her mother rest her head on his sister's shoulder and knew that her mother shared the amusement, the fondness in addition to her married love for him, that her mother belonged with these people who remembered his youth.

She remembered a story about him, a story which her mother, never him, had shared with her. When his own mother had died of tuberculosis when he was ten, he had sat by her bedside day after day. His father had been stern, his siblings older than he, and he had adored his pretty, kind mother. So he had sat by her bedside until she died.

Daisy cried, then, as much for that boy as for the man who had been her father.

Decoration Day

T heir old name for Memorial Day slipped into her mind
as Edith Ingram, a woman of many years, sat on the
steep hillside and watched her sister and mother below,
cleaning her grandmother's grave and placing upon it the
plastic flowers her sister had bought at Wal-Mart. Décor-
ation Day. In her Kentucky childhood, they had made the
flowers. Her mother's long callused fingers would pull the
edge of a scissors blade taut across pieces of crinkly pink or
red or white crepe paper until they curved into rose petals.
Edith, the oldest child, had been allowed to wrap the strips
of green paper along the wire stem.

Now, half a century later, Edith stretched out her
fingers to touch her father's grave, wishing that they had
brought crepe flowers or real ones planted in pots. Beneath
a cloudless sky, the thickly leaved trees that surrounded the
graveyard made of it a peninsula: the world seemed linked

to it only by the vertical dirt road that began down below at her father's birthplace and then ran up, up, past houses folded into shelves dug from the hill, until it reached the graveyard. His youngest sister lived in the birthplace now, and the houses on the hillside belonged to Edith's cousins.

Yesterday morning she had flown into mid-Ohio from New York. The sister who had married a Columbus boy she met at Ohio State came to the airport to greet her and take her to their mother's house, the house to which the family had moved from Kentucky when Edith was twelve. It was near a country town, forty minutes away from the glass factory where their father had worked until a piece of machinery had fallen on him and crushed his back.

For many years now, Edith had been alone in the city; her companionship limited to well-mannered friends who had their own solitudes or troubled relationships to manage. She still recognized in herself something eager that she attributed to the Kentucky girl bereft of her rightful destiny, the hills and the long chain of kinfolk who had been left behind. In her adult relations with people, Edith had become circumspect, her hidden eagerness a threat of disruption. This circumspection, this loneliness was defeated only by the voices of her mother and certain of her siblings. In her conversations with them, a southern sound entered her speech, and her voice registered heights and depths that she had not expressed in New York since the divorce from her young husband and perhaps not even before her marriage. For his imperfect love, Edith had substituted the intensities of her profession as an architect. She gained a certain satisfaction from the structures on which she labored, though she had been convinced until recently that she would never get to see the buildings whose sketches lay hidden away in a drawer in her apartment. She spent a great deal of time on the telephone with her family.

On this Decoration Day, then, after the long trip south to Kentucky, Edith Ingram sat beside her father's grave. The spring wind sped thickly leaved trees, and the hills beyond rose into a sky so blue that it could have been a memory of Heaven—the blue felt cutout pressed against a large easel used by the traveling Bible teachers who had come to her childhood school. The hills' own darker blue seemed a vision of some possible future. She felt that her father was at home here, back in the hills. Birds sang in the trees, and the forms of her mother and sister moved below.

Edith had been thinking much of her father lately. She had been offered a chance to design a small-town museum in Connecticut, and in the way that people will, she had said to the invisible air, "Well, Daddy, this one is for you." Once her parents had come to visit her in New York. By then, she had had her West Side apartment, with its arched doorways and a view of the Hudson. To her surprise, her father had enjoyed New York. Having forgotten much, having taken on the obtuse mantle of her bourgeois life, she had forgotten how adventurous he was and how eager when his interest was aroused. She stood waiting for her parents to go past her and out the door so that she could lock it behind them before she led them to Chinatown. He was on crutches. With his blue eyes, he looked at her directly, cogently. Love and adult judgment mingled in the look.

An image of her six-year-old hand in his on a spring evening in Kentucky. Here and there on the dark hills, lights flutter in a light wind. They are going up the dirt road to the one-room schoolhouse where Hollywood movies are shown on Friday nights during warm weather. Mommy has stayed behind with the younger children. They both know that the other will enjoy the movie. They both feel guilty about leaving the others behind.

He had tried to keep his family safe by ruling it and by keeping its members at home but had been unable to restrain his oldest daughter's desire to have adventures.

On a certain Saturday in Ohio, Edith and her father had been hoeing the small cornfield where they grew "eating" corn and corn for the chickens. Her brothers had gone into the woods to find fuel for the kitchen stove, and her sisters were working in the garden. Edith hated hoeing corn, the hot sweat and sameness of it, the humped back. A garter snake had found its way into her left shoe the past summer. Silently mutinous, she bent her head and her back, not even trying to match her father's swift, efficient hoe. He was silent, too. He had been laid off that summer.

At the end of the row, he dropped down beneath the huge old oak tree at the far end. There was a gallon jar of water there, still with a little ice in it. "Come on," he said. "You can finish your row later." Gratefully she had dropped the hoe on the sun-grayed dirt and hurried for the shade, a sweat bee or two undoubtedly stinging her on the way. From where they sat, Edith could see the cool pond and the butterfly bushes flowering on the slope. The pleasant drone of bugs, the occasional call of a bird. Nature was the home they had carried with them.

He said, "You see that creek over there. I'm thinking about settin' me up a still back on in there. Make some money."

She had just won a state prize in Ohio history and got recognized by the DAR as a good citizen (purely on the grounds of her straight A's).

"You can't do that," she cried.

"We got to get out of the hole," he said heavily.

"You can't do that. It's illegal. It's awful anyhow, making

moonshine."

"You don't tell me what to do, young lady." He rose to his feet and dismissed her, returning silently to the hoe. He had never built the still. Probably her mother had begged him not to.

Edith Ingram thought of her father's childhood, the death of his father in the mines, the death of his mother by TB, the boy shunted from family to family, families who themselves were scrabbling to survive. She had wished for years that she had said, "Go ahead, Daddy. Anything I can do?"

Returning from college to the big shabby house with all its shady nooks sat in the middle of a small wood— returning, she had said to her mother, "How can he go hunting bobwhites? What have they ever done to him?"

"It's food," the brother who was next to her in age said scornfully, overhearing. "You think something don't die when you eat a chicken? You don't remember wringing a chicken's neck?"

Only once had Edith heard her father cry. She had come home from college a newborn political animal and had made fun of his presidential candidate. He had shouted at her, and she had shouted back. Her mother cried, "You two will be the death of me." It was an unhappy year for the family. One sister had been very ill, and one brother hadn't been allowed to join the basketball team even though he was a very good player. Her father had been working overtime almost every night in the glass factory. His paycheck was still too slender to buy adequate school clothes for Edith's younger brothers and sisters. (Edith was taking out national defense loans to eke out her scholarship.) The sound of his rough, smothered sobs leaked out of her parents' bedroom into the frightened house. Her mother came to her and whispered fiercely, "Don't you ever talk to him that way again."

A tiny green worm inched its way over his grave. It was a pretty thing and seemed to signify some amelioration of the usual worm/grave relationship. Edith Ingram's mother and sister were impatiently beckoning her. They were almost finished with her grandmother's grave. The three of them had begun with husband and father, with the broad arching head-stone that spanned not only his place but the flat empty space where Edith's mother would lie. Her name was already engraved on the stone, leaving only the date to be entered. From that grave, they had moved to the tiny grave of her mother's true firstborn, burst sightless from the womb of a seventeen-year-old girl. Then to the graves of her father's long-dead brother and sister, and finally to his parents' graves, headed by the deep red stones her father had bought in a good year to replace thin slabs of leaning rock. The family legend said that when his mother was dying, the little boy of six ran away from home. He had by that time already seen the lifeless bodies of his father and a sister with whom he had played.

Like a gift, there came to Edith now a scene from a few years after her father's accident. The young woman is coming home from the city. It is shortly after her divorce, about which momentarily she is feeling a pure relief from the absence of trouble. On the plane, she had—in those days before cigarettes were forbidden—pleasurably smoked one of those long brown cigarettes of Virginia tobacco that she favored, and she had had a vodka and tonic. Both of these substances had been abhorred by her mother and forbidden by her father (who himself liked a big cigar and indulged in rare drinking sprees). This taboo had been lifted for her brothers when they graduated from high school, but it was still in effect for the daughters. It was unhappily accepted that Edith broke the taboo, though many head shakings and an air of restraint attended this acceptance.

Smoking a long brown cigarette, then, and fashionable in her Bloomingdale's dress, Edith alights from the plane, where she is greeted by a silent, warm-eyed brother and a chattering sister who grab her luggage and tell her that yet another sister will be getting married in September and that yet another brother has his brand-new child. All the world is early summer as her brother's red Corvette—which he bought cheap in a static condition and brought to perfection with that tinkering ability he inherited from his father—as the red Corvette makes its way out into the splendid Ohio countryside, rocking with flowers and cows and memories.

The car pulls into the wood where their parents live. Her mother is in the kitchen cooking enough for an army of thousands, aided by yet another sister. Edith hugs them and is hugged in return. "Happy birthday," her mother says.

"Where's Daddy?" Edith asks.

"Out on the back porch stringing beans."

With terror and love, Edith spies on her crippled father from the screened doorway. His melancholy eyes half shut, his large gnarled fingers painfully stringing beans from the garden. Her terror is a prophetic sense of loss, which he dismisses with a glance as he smiles at her. "You home? It's about time."

At Edith's birthday request, her mother has prepared a dinner of fried chicken and mashed potatoes and biscuits and gravy and green beans. There are eight of them sitting along the table that he had made long ago. Sun floods through the windows, and fresh country air sweetly butters Edith's nostrils. They relax into their common history. "And Daddy," they say. "Daddy strung the beans."

The birthday cake, unrelievedly chocolate, is brought out, and everyone sings "Happy Birthday" to Edith, half of them out of tune. Everyone has little presents for her. A pen set, a scarf, a potholder crocheted by her mother. Her father's present is in a long thin box that looks like, could it be? It is. A carton of her Virginia cigarettes. Edith gets up and kisses his cheek, a gesture that she knows will both please and discomfort him.

As she rose now to join her mother and sister, Edith Ingram was thinking of a dream that, in her twenties, she had dreamed frequently. She is in a wood, trying desperately to get back to her childhood home in Kentucky. Along the creek, by the overhanging hazelnut bushes, she runs up against barbed wire. There is a red-painted sign that says "Entrance forbidden."

She would place the last plastic flower on her grandmother's grave, and they would go down to her father's sister's house. Then they would get back into the car, and the hills would twang plangently in the twilight as they left. The other night she had dreamed that dream again. Her father appeared dressed in his work clothes. He held the wire up while she rolled under, and then she was home free.

Blackberry Picking

Noah and Joy Linn decided to move back to Osier County, home to Kentucky after somebody shot the miner who lived in the last house at the other end of the coal camp. They were sitting on their front porch on the first pretty April day—all of them—and Elsie was helping her brother Chad with his spelling homework while Jody and Dennis quarreled over the red ball. May slept in her mother's lap. Even in the coal camp—where they had lived now for two years, their eyes turned back to Sarvis Creek while they went about the motions of living—spring looked lovely on the opposite mountain. The redbuds were in bloom, their muted flame like a small song beyond the slag pile which lay directly across the railroad track. The gray houses of the camp were softened by the spring light and the pale blue sheen of the sky.

Elsie turned from Chad's book to her own. She had an

arithmetic test coming up, and Mrs. Engelbert was tough and mean. She had to be, Noah said, because of all the big boys who were in the sixth-grade class. They cursed a lot, and some of them smoked cigarettes behind the schoolhouse.

Elsie had won the spelling bee, but when she went to the county seat to compete against spellers from other schools, she got nervous and soon had to sit down. Joy Linn was almost as disappointed as she was because Elsie might have got to go to the National Spelling Bee in Washington, and Joy Linn wanted her to have that. Joy Linn's ambition for her children had developed when they left Sarvis Creek and came to West Virginia to the coal camp. Elsie heard her tell Noah one night that she didn't want her children growing up in such a place. "Aaaah, honey," Elsie's father said. "We got to eat." "I know, I know," Joy Linn said. "I know you do the best you can."

Suddenly, as they sat on the front porch that April day, there was a loud noise. Noah jumped up. "That's a gun," he said. "What damn fool is huntin' this close to the camp. Git inside, all of you."

But just at that moment, the miner, still with a black face from his day's work, lurched into view, and as he stumbled, another shot rang out, and he fell down.

"Git inside. *Now,*" Noah said. Elsie watched through the lace curtains while her father went off the porch and down the road. What if he gets shot, she thought, and her stomach got upset. Joy Linn had put May in the crib and was standing beside Elsie, clutching her daughter's shoulder.

When Noah got back, he said it was all a drunken argument over an old car. He looked at Joy Linn. "That settles it," he said. "We're gittin' the young'uns to hell out of here."

"Where we goin'?" Joy Linn asked tremulously.

"We're going home."

So they returned to Kentucky, but not to the white frame house on Sarvis Creek (the white frame house in the garden, by the brown creek, beneath the hill, where all the children except May had been born) because somebody else, one of the Telcotts, had rented it. The only job Noah had been able to find was one hauling coal for a yellow-dog outfit. He thought he might get a union job over at Brandy in a few months.

The house to which they moved was unpainted and small, sitting on the hill above the railroad track. The chicken house and the toilet were up on the hill above, and Joy Linn shook her head. "It ain't sanitary," she said to Noah, who shook his head. "Best we can do for right now," he answered.

They bought some White Rocks for the chicken house, mostly layers, one red-combed rooster, and a few fryers. Uncle Jeremiah let them have a garden on his adjoining property, up on the flat out of sight of the house. "The coons and rabbits will eat it up," Joy Linn said, but Noah replied, "It'll be all right. I know a trick or two worth knowin'."

And there were the hills. Home. Elsie went into the woods for hours alone, returning with her arms full. She started a rock collection and took a book on pressing flowers out of the school library. Joy Linn laughed. "There's plenty more where that come from," she teased. "You gonna gather all the flowers and pick up all the rocks." Elsie shook her head. She did not want to say that maybe the time would come again when she would not be here. Saying it might make it come true.

It was early summer, and one day Aunt Gladys came by to get Elsie. On her way, she had picked up Uncle Jeremiah and Aunt Wilma's two girls, the cousins with whom Elsie walked to school and in the evening played tag and Anthony-over-the-barn. It was blackberry picking time. Buckets knocked together while Gladys and the cousins shifted about in the yard, their shoes covered with mud from last night's rain. Gladys was already wiping the sweat off her forehead with the back of her hand. "Come on, Elsie," Katie called. Elsie didn't want to go blackberry picking. She was rereading the book about a beautiful heiress in love with a mysterious captain. Her mother spoke impatiently from the kitchen. Reluctantly Elsie got into her jeans and took the bucket from Joy Linn's hand.

The noonday fire in the cook stove hadn't died down yet. On the radio, Bill Monroe was singing "Blue moon of Kentucky." May ran in the back door from the yard where the other children were playing softball. "I want to go with Elsie," she shouted. Joy Linn pushed aside a pile of beans and picked her up. "Then who'd keep me company?" Legs anchored about her mother's waist, the baby sucked her thumb and watched Elsie thread shoe laces.

Elsie's naked feet sweated inside her shoes.

They left the road, walking up through knee-high broomsage. Katie talked about the boy she had a yen for. "He's got the biggest old shoulders." Gladys twisted her head, smiling to say that Katie was brash. *Brash, blasted,* Elsie thought. When she tried out the curse words used by girls at school, Noah told her to hush her dirty mouth. Blasted berries were the small dry ones. "Oh, blasted," Elsie would mutter and, seeing Joy Linn's eyes on her, "berry." Smile on her mother's lips.

They got out of the broomsage under the tall trees. It was cool there. Gladys bent over some white flowers. "I never seed none like this afore. You girls know what they are?" Nobody knew. The sun fluttered on Gladys's red hair.

For months she had gone around with a pale tight face talking on and on about how she couldn't get compensation from the mine where Uncle George got killed.

(They had come over from the coal camp home to Kentucky to visit Papaw and Mamaw. "Well, looky here," Mamaw said. "It's my other daughter come to roost." "Where's Gladys and George," Joy Linn asked. "You s'pose they didn't see us drive up? I seed a boy out playin' in the yard. Thought it must be Billy Dean."

Mamaw rubbed her hands back and forth in her apron. "Didn't you git my letter?"

"What letter, Mommy?"

"George was killed in the mines about a month ago," Papaw said, looking at the ceiling. "We thought you all would make it to the funeral."

"We didn't know," Joy Linn said, pressing her lips.

"Slate fall," Papaw said. "Crushed his chest. Got two other men, too."

"Didn't even touch his face," Mamaw added. "Gladys is sleeping all the time. Feeds Billy Dean on sandwiches and pop. Let's go over and git her and Billy Dean now." Papaw and Noah killed and plucked a chicken. Mamaw rolled the pieces in corn-meal while Joy Linn peeled potatoes. The kitchen wallpaper was yellow with tiny red flowers. Papaw had put too much coal in the stove, and the caps were red hot, but a cool wind blew off the hill through the open window. Gladys didn't seem very glad to see them. When she brought out the funeral pictures, Billy Dean went outside. Elsie peeked at the first one and saw a stiff figure resting on draped white satin. It seemed to her that somehow he had died because they had moved away.)

Now that Gladys was being courted by Jim Barnes, she laughed a lot again. Gold flickered in her eyes. She and Billy

Dean had moved to a ramshackle house over on Pleasant Ridge. They spent a lot of time cutting down trees, clearing underbrush, and planting a garden and a cornfield. Her hands closed on the flower stems were red and scaly.

Trees gave way to the big flat where the blackberries were. They walked cautiously, trying to avoid the sawberry vines that made ugly little scratches on bare ankles. Gladys stopped to catch her breath, and the girls waited. Looking down the hill, Elsie saw her house. Up on Sarvis Mountain across the tracks sat Mamaw and Papaw's big white house. A little smoke still rose from her own chimney. Her brothers and sisters were still playing in the backyard. Chickens fought over the corn that Joy Linn was scattering. A blue jay shrilled behind her. The rest of the world was silent.

With a loud commotion, a train loomed through the gap. Elsie strained to see the faces passing by, but the train was too far away. Gladys stirred. "We're almost there."

The blackberry vines rose from a clump of half-rotten logs and rocks—big juicy berries. "Shit," Katie said. "It'll take us all day to pick them vines."

"Hush your mouth," Gladys snapped. "You know your ma wouldn't like that word."

Berries plopped softly into tin buckets. Elsie wiped the sweat off her face. As she rubbed her hand on the jeans, a sweat bee, pinioned between thumb and jeans, stung her, dying. She could feel the juice drying at the corners of her mouth. Her hands were already purple.

Ethel giggled. "Elsie's got on purple lipstick."

"You go git a looking glass and look at your ownself."

Gladys was off to one side picking, her first bucket about a quarter full. Elsie looked down at her own. The bottom wasn't much more than covered. She picked steadily, putting every berry in the bucket.

Katie screamed, jumping back. "There's a snake in there. It's a rattlesnake."

Gladys picked up the sharp-bladed hoe, cautiously parting the vines with it. "It's leaving."

"I don't care. I won't pick another berry."

"Well, I can't say as I blame you much. Let's move on to the next patch."

The sun blasted them. Gladys and Katie went right into the middle of the vines while Elsie and Ethel picked on the edges. Their clothes stuck to their bodies. Elsie began to notice the tiny bugs running over the berries. She dropped a berry carrying a spider that ran onto her finger and up her arm before she could flick it off.

Skirting a cliff, they heard men and dogs. Gladys shook her head. "Sounds like Foster Elberts and his boys." Noah had ordered Elsie never to speak to the Elberts boys. "They're bad news," he declared. "Ever last one of 'em. Devil's own seed." Foster had killed his daddy with an ax in a drunken argument over twenty dollars. He had been sent up for it, but they let him out in a few years.

Dogs suddenly seemed to be running downhill. Men were laughing. "Run, girls, run," Gladys shouted. "Foster's sikked the hounds on us."

Elsie had seen a dog chew at a dead possum.

On the way down, she tried to keep up with Katie, passing Ethel, who had fallen down. Gladys stopped, taking something out of her apron pocket. "Run on, girls, git outa my way."

They passed on by, and then Elsie turned around. Her aunt had gotten down on one knee. She was pointing a pistol straight up the hill. She pulled the trigger. The noise made a deafening film across Elsie's ears, running jarringly out into trees. Above them, voices cursed. Somebody called,

"Here Charlie, here boy; here Black, here boy here." The baying hushed. Gladys said to her staring niece, "They'd have called them back ennyways; they'd have called them back, honey." Elsie stares at the gun in her aunt's hand. "It was too far for a pistol ennyway," Aunt Gladys said. She dropped the gun. "It was your Uncle George's gun. I hunted it out after he got killed. I thought maybe I'd go and shoot them murderin' bosses." Elsie stared. "Don't look at me like that, child. Go on down the hill and join your cousins. I'll be right behind." Looking down the hill to where Katie had collapsed against the pasture fence, now that the danger had ended, Elsie found herself doubling over with laughter.

Encounters
of a Close Kind

H er brother said, his broad masculine face intent upon
the road, "Is there anybody else you'd like to visit
while we're down there?" They were traveling from Ohio to
the hills of eastern Kentucky, where Kate had not been since
their father's funeral in 1990, a three-day affair, shocking to
her in its fundamental Baptist oratorical grief. She had once
before attended a family funeral when she was six—a great-
uncle had died, and his wife had wailed all the way to the
graveyard, but other than that detail, she had forgotten
what it was like. At their father's funeral, one of the three
preachers, a nephew of his, their cousin, had sternly hinted
that the elegy, written by Kate, the eldest, was all too short.
Kate thought she had managed to say a lot in those few
grief-ridden sentences, but Osier County funerals were

given to more obvious farewells.

Her brother, Emory, named for his father, was working diligently on a genealogy of the family. He had been busy with it for two years now and had made visits to archives and courthouses and called relatives, including several whom none of them had previously known. And Kate did not know Emory, her youngest brother, very well. When Kate had left home for college, wild with excitement and willfully detaching herself from the family, Emory had been three. The family story, one of those well-worn stories that get repeated over and over in certain family situations, was that he had tried to call her on the telephone, and the operator (they had operators in those days) had been mean to him.

Like the rest of their large family, they had chosen different paths. Kate had been in her way adventurous, running off to New York in her early twenties and getting hired for a lowly position by an elegant magazine (her heart intent on becoming a professional writer), moving up slowly and eventually returning to student life, in Chicago, in her late thirties. The financial outcome of all this had been an ill-paying copyediting job at an academic publisher. Recently retired, hoping to write full-time, but finding herself unfit to subsist on Social Security, Kate had increasingly taken on freelance editing work. As she entered her seventies, she still found writing crucial, though emotionally difficult and unremunerative. ("Are you *still* submitting?" asked a former New York friend from the old days incredulously, half-pitying, half-admiring such tenacity.)

Emory had undertaken an engineering career with great tenacity and spirit, practically living on peanut butter in college. (Kate heard this from her mother. She herself was long gone then, living in New York and getting involved with an intense, unstable man who demanded most of her attention.) But, after having become so successful an engineer that he had worked on the Hoover Dam and been sent to Australia, Emory had left his career to start a business, which he sold in turn when it turned out to be highly marketable. As they made their way along Mountain Parkway, lined right now with flowering locust trees, Kate wondered if he ever missed engineering.

He had then turned to raising his two sons while his attractive Southern wife continued as a high-powered executive. Kate had attended their wedding, held in an expensive reception venue which the groom and bride had paid for themselves. They had gone to Paris for their honeymoon. (There was in the house of Kate and Emory's mother an enchanting wedding picture of two handsome, happy young people.) They now lived in the Florida panhandle, near Pensacola. Kate had never been to visit, though Emory had come to Chicago with their mother to see Kate receive her Ph.D., and then he had brought his two boys to see the city. They had spent six hours in the Museum of Science and Industry, and Kate had had almost as much fun as Emory and his young sons, the oldest of whom was now graduating from college.

While Kate's childhood had been spent in the hills of eastern Kentucky, Emory had been born and raised in Ohio. His sister was bemused by and slightly envious of this sibling who had gone farther than any of them toward achieving the American Dream. Though she knew by now that the well-off did not lead charmed lives, she yet envied Emory his trips abroad, his wife's casual visits to New York, even his free time, which had increased as his sons grew older and which he used for his genealogy, for reading widely, and for amassing and watching a large film collection.

(There was a home theater in his capacious basement. Capacious on the report of their mother.)

Like relearning a difficult lesson, Kate was now proudly interested in her family and their varied doings. The brother next in age to Kate and dear to her heart was a subsistence farmer, quiet, warring with daydreams and nightmares. Then came the sister in Vermont who had married and divorced an academic and gone back to school to become a professor herself, and following her came the sister who was an insurance company executive living in and loving California. Two other sisters, a teacher and an office manager, had married husbands who turned out to have an aptitude for success. A third brother was a factory worker, a voracious reader, and suspicious of success. Next to Emory in attaining financial success and, Kate hoped, career satisfaction was the youngest of them all, a sister who was a dedicated software developer. Most of them had children, and the children had had children, and these, in turn, had more children. Family reunions were enormous and noisy.

Emory said, "What year did Aunt Gracie die? Was it 2005?"

"I think it was 2000," Kate replied, searching in the increasing fog of recent memories. She thought of the Vermont sister, who also dabbled in genealogy. "Let's call Jenny." As she punched in her sister's number, she had some feeling of guilt and estrangement, as though she and Jenny and Emory were exhibiting some class camaraderie that separated them from the others. Jenny said, "I went to the funeral, remember? She was my favorite aunt. It was 2004."

The Corlisses were all heavily invested in memory, attached to the image of their father, a miner who had been difficult and lovable and finally disabled and then dead, and they were also attached to a Kentucky-biased childhood which they did not know what to do with. This applied to Emory as well, even though he and Natasha, the youngest, were technically Ohioans. Most of them, including Kate, adored their mother. Although Priscilla Corliss was now in her nineties and suffering from a stroke and macular degeneration, among other things, she remained the center of family life, with the help of Natasha, whom Kate had been allowed to name. Kate had been reading *War and Peace* at the time.

Emory was especially close to Mrs. Corliss. He spoke now, and Kate looked over at his good-looking face and stocky figure, thinking how much he resembled their father, his namesake, though he was brown-eyed and brown-haired (turning a little gray). Their father had had curly black hair and blue eyes, a combination not inherited by any of his children. "How long are you staying at Mom's?" Emory asked.

"Until her birthday," Kate answered. "That place on her leg may be cancerous, too, so maybe I'll be back down before long, though." Kate still lived in Chicago, but she had been spending several weeks in Ohio in an effort, laden with equal parts of love and guilt, to temporarily ease Natasha's life and to provide daily company to their mother, who was depressed. This was not Kate's thing. As the eldest sister in a large and poor family, she had had a short childhood and fled further responsibility when she went off to college. She had somewhere along the way (she preferred not to be detailed about this) had a bout of mental illness and considered in her darker moments that she had used this condition as an excuse to avoid further entanglement with the needy human race—until she thought of the man of her New York years and knew she had not been wholly successful.

That relationship had been lengthy and demanding. Now somehow, all these years later, she had become hooked again by the human race, caught by traitor emotions.

Emory was saying, "How long has her memory been this bad?"

"It was the stroke, Emory. It deteriorated after the stroke."

"Yes, I guess so," he said somberly, regretfully. "I couldn't come up because that was shortly after I had my operation." He had had his gall bladder removed, and now he had put on some weight. Not a lot but enough to make him resemble his father even more. "I have to have another hip operation next month." She looked at him thoughtfully, thinking now about how she teased him about spending so long in the bathroom mornings. It wasn't all vanity (of which she had her own share), probably, but an effort to keep the world straight, on an even keel. She realized she could sometimes tell when speaking to him that there were things that he was uncertain about, like his considerable intellectual prowess and his position as a raiser of sons. How deep did those insecurities run? Did they approach her own constant self-questioning?

They were getting off the Mountain Parkway now, heading for U.S. 23, which was the main artery for several Kentucky counties, heading in the direction of the invisible hamlet of Sweet Branch, their father's home deep in the hills, past which they would be going later in the day. The last time Kate had been there, she was twelve and what she remembered most were two men who had stopped the car by the simple process of jumping in front of it (an easy feat as it lurched up a muddy, rutted road) and who had known their father and had made threatening gestures. It had been winter then, and the car windows were closed, so Kate could not hear what the three men were saying. When Emory Senior got back in the car, he said merely, to their mother and in a tone that brooked no further discussion, "Just two of the Boyden boys. I'll tell you later." In the back seat, Natasha squirming in her lap, Kate found her fear had changed to fuming curiosity. In family stories, the Boydens were known for their lawlessness, and her father had once been a deputy sheriff. She wondered if their anger arose from that fact or whether they had merely been drinking. Recently something had reminded her of this incident, and she asked her mother about it, but the latter no longer remembered. Most of her children's young years had been spent among *her* family, a social cut above her husband's, with more teachers and carpenters and store owners than miners. Their manners were genteel in, Kate thought, mostly a good way but did include some degree of snobbism, and she wondered now, as she had wondered before, if their father had felt this.

They were getting close now. Kate suddenly saw a line of cliffs with huge clusters of purple and lilac-colored flowers hanging down richly, like the Deep South. She did not remember ever having seen them in this part of her world. Had she forgotten something so beautiful, so lush, or was this something new? It was almost an affront. "Is that wisteria," she asked Emory. "Heck if I know," he answered briefly, concentrating on his driving. He was passing a large, grimy coal truck. Themselves now inhabitants of urban sprawl, they were in the country. The traffic had increased a little as they neared Osierville, the town where their family had conducted its special businesses like getting a bank loan or going into the hospital, and they laughed simultaneously and with real appreciation when they saw the sign "Congested Area Ahead."

Then, following the Google map that Emory had handed her to navigate with, they took the indicated exit and were in Osierville. Kate could recount on the fingers of one hand the times she remembered having been in the town itself. It looked so small now, cut off abruptly by the hills on every side. They rode along brief residential streets and then into downtown. Emory, who had never before visited Osierville, pointed out an attractive-looking courthouse that Kate did not remember. "The hotel is next door to the library," he said, having as always done his research, just as she saw a large sign saying "Osier County Public Library." They turned right, and there was the hotel. Emory had found it online, and she had been, considering the location, somewhat taken aback by the cost. Having done some minor research of her own, however, before she made her reservation, she was reassured by the fact that this was a well-known interstate chain and further by the fact that nobody had reported bedbugs. Right now, these were preoccupying the nation's travelers, having swarmed up out of some hinterland of the past.

Inside the hotel, Kate was bemused by the combination of urban comfort and the drawls of the hotel people, which to her sounded like the country voices of her childhood. It seemed a contradiction in terms, and she wanted to ask them if they lived here in town or went home to the hollers. But, though she might be in Osierville, the mythic town of memory, she saw and heard that the clerks behind the desk—who probably were not called clerks—were professionals and busy with incoming and outgoing guests. The hotel was near a small private university, and Kate heard a woman with a Midwestern twang discussing with a companion her son's junior year.

Emory's room was on the second floor, while hers was

on the fourth. She felt some combination of adventure and unease when he got off the elevator, and she proceeded on her own. She had not had a great deal of occasion to spend time in hotels, and here she was in Osierville nervously inserting a twenty-first-century key card.

Kate and Emory's first stop was to be the graveyard belonging to their mother's family, located on property now belonging to a reclusive first cousin whom they had not seen for decades. When their mother had been able, she and some one or two or three of her children had brought crepe flowers to the graveyard on Memorial Day, which she still sometimes called Decoration Day, but no one ever saw the cousin, though they visited his sister, who lived further up the hill, just below the graveyard and was gently sociable.

They meant to snatch a cup of coffee before resuming their travels on U.S. 23, but it was Easter, and the two restaurants they passed were closed. It was a rainy morning. Mist rose on the hills in that well-remembered (by Kate) way so that they saw the green and intermittently flowering hillsides through a film of mist and light rain. Kate spoke impulsively to her brother, "We are in one of the world's most beautiful landscapes." He nodded sympathetically. No mountaintop removal or strip mining had yet touched this particular spot, though they had seen a horrendous strip mine on the way down, all rust and mud in the rain, and they had seen too a truncated mountain, its remainder like a butchered thumb covered over with an acid-looking green. Kate wondered how the drinking water was in that valley. What had happened to the people who had inhabited its filled-in hollow? Where did they go?

Having gone past Copper Road, a narrow, black-topped way that led to their mother's childhood and to the graveyard, they had to turn around at another small road and come back. This time Kate thought she recognized the huge old maple tree that marked the turning. It is my childhood, too, she told herself, knowing that she was exaggerating, that they had moved away time and again, moved away and come back and moved away again.

The road dipped down to a treacherous-looking bridge, concrete over wood pilings, and she looked north to where the swinging bridge had been. Of course, it was gone. Had been gone for years. Their grandparents' house was gone too, the house that used to be a feed store, where in their mother's childhood, when the family still lived in the old home place, still green and lovely somewhere on the edges of memory, people had come to get their corn ground, their sugar cane turned into molasses. And their great-grandfather's general store (he had owned the feed store too) across the way was also gone, the store where Kate used to play, where their father had first noticed their mother as she clerked behind the wooden counter. As she grew older, Mrs. Corliss reminisced more and more about those days, telling stories that her children had never before heard.

Past the bridge, then, and across the railroad, where the steam locomotives used to let out their long-drawn whistles, and there had been the peopled windows of passenger trains to watch, turning left, past houses where cousins lived, and then right, up the steep incline that led to the graveyard. They stopped at the last house before the graveyard, where their cousin Elsie lived, offspring of a union between their father's sister and their mother's uncle. Kate had played with Elsie and her sisters one summer when the family had lived on Copper Road. Elsie and her husband were holding for them the flowers that Emory had bought by phone from a local florist who was kin to their father. The husband came to the door, wearing a rumpled t-shirt and old jeans and smoking a cigarette. Kate, who had met him only twice, briefly, suddenly could not remember his name. She could smell the fug of old cigarette smoke in the living room beyond him. All the shades were pulled in the middle of the day. "Good to see you, Bill," Emory said.

"Elsie's not doing well," Bill said. "She's been sick." They sat down in the dark room, Kate on a comfortable couch whose gray-and-maroon color she could barely see. Emory perched alertly on a matching chair. He had been in touch with Elsie and Bill during his genealogy research, and Bill greeted him like a buddy.

There was movement in the dim recess to the right, and Elsie joined them. Kate was shocked by her cousin's appearance, comparing this gaunt woman with straggling gray hair, dressed in a thin, rumpled robe, to the remembered slim, erect girl with luminous gray eyes. In her illness, Elsie's face had become birdlike. Holding a smoking cigarette of her own, she greeted Kate now with great, sad warmth, "Well, it's Katie," she said, looking directly into Kate's eyes. "Your mother said you'd be coming along with Emory here, but I said I'll believe it when I see it." She hugged Kate tightly, and Kate found herself hugging back and meaning it. Elsie had lost her first husband to a mining accident and, recently, a son to cancer. Kate had met that husband two or three times, the son only once. "Lord, honey. You remember that year you and Aunt Gladys and Ethel and me went all over these hills."

"I remember, Elsie," Kate responded, her voice developing something of a drawl and twang that would have surprised her northern friends. "Remember when we went berry picking."

"Lord, do I remember *that*. That old Foster Elberts and his boys sikked their dogs on us. Aunt Gladys was with us, and she dropped down on her right knee and pulled a gun. And you went running down the hill so fast, saying 'the Devil take the hind piece,' which would have disgraced Aunt Priscilla, and I got tickled and just stood there laughing after Gladys shot."

"I got 'the Devil take the hind piece' from Daddy's cousins over in Sweet Branch," Kate said half-defensively.

"Aunt Gladys's dead now, Katie. Died of cancer of the throat four years ago this month. Her and Ethel and me were real sorry when your family moved back to West Virginia."

So many people here seemed to have cancer. Was it because mining had polluted those clear, cold streams? "Not half as sorry as I was," Kate said. "Mommy told me about Gladys's death."

Hoping to lighten the atmosphere, Kate turned to hear what Emory and Bill were talking about. Bill was doing the talking, and he was talking about hunting deer and coons. "My brother Johnny owns a cabin at Cave Run, up in Menafee County, right on the lake. Our son Junior comes with Elsie and me, and we canoe and fish and hunt—all but Elsie, she leaves the hunting part to us. This year we ain't felt like going yet. Elsie's got this here thyroid problem, and I got arthritis real bad in my back and legs."

Emory asked, "Isn't Menafee up near Lexington?" Kate had been at Cave Run once when visiting a friend who taught at Morehead.

"It's still a good piece to Lexington, but, yeah, it's real closer than we are here. Some Lexington people have cabins at the lake and even a Louisville couple. We're afraid the next thing to come is visitors from elsewhere, and the lake starts getting developed." It was a wild place, Cave Run, despite its cabins. You stood on the narrow rocky beach and dabbled your toes in the cold deep water while tangled forest pressed at your back. There were frogs and huge turtles and huge bass in the lake and a myriad of other, smaller fish. If you made your way into the forest, not such an easy thing to do, you might come across a deer blind. Looking around at the hills surrounding her cousin's house, Kate thought that going to Cave Run was a kind of busman's holiday. Didn't they ever feel the urge to go somewhere urban?

They sat there for half an hour longer, talking of ill-health and of Elsie's dead parents and scattered siblings. Emory stood up and said, "Well, we'd better go. We're only here for today and tomorrow, and we need to visit the two graveyards today." Bill pointed them toward the crumbling storehouse where he had put the flowers. As Kate and Elsie were hugging goodbye, Kate looked beyond her cousin, beyond the dark room, into the kitchen, where brilliant Kentucky sunshine splintered on the old appliances like a hope. She wondered if she would ever see Elsie again.

Fortunately, the rain had stopped. Emory had bought tons of flowers, crosses and wreaths, and single flowers, red and pink and blue and yellow flowers. "I got what I thought Mom would like," he said. (Mrs. Corliss preferred paper flowers to the real thing because, in Kate's childhood, paper flowers had been a family art practiced each May by the women, who sat on Mamaw's back porch and fashioned them of wire and crepe paper.) Emory had bought enough flowers to decorate thickly their father's grave and their maternal grandmother's and those of their twin brothers who had never seen daylight and one of their uncles, dead at age three. (There had been a divorce, and Papaw, who had then married a younger woman, notably a redhead such as Mamaw had once been, was buried elsewhere. In that generation of Kentucky Baptists, divorce was still scandalous, and for years afterward, some of Mrs. Corliss's siblings would not speak to their father. Mamaw had been tragic.)

They piled the flowers in the back of Emory's van and retook their seats. The road up looked narrow, muddy, and dangerous, the van slipping a little first here and then there near the steep edge. It was mercifully a very short trip. Emory parked on a grassy verge near the edge because there was not much room. Kate sighed with relief as they got out, wondering as always how they would manage to get turned around for the trip down. The familiar graveyard with its sparse grasses showed one new grave, its bare dirt decorated only with a pot of geraniums and a headstone with more writing than usual. She could not read it from beside the van. Emory carefully extracted from the van the crosses and wreaths on their wire tripods and handed them to her to erect on the wet grass. Each grabbing as well a handful of loose flowers, they made their way to the upper part of the graveyard where Emory Corliss Senior lay. The headstone extended to his left, where there was a space for his wife. Kate's breath caught at the view of soft gray sky and green hills. She thought as she thought each time she came, that she must arrange for her own death, to be cremated and her ashes strewn here.

They had forgotten to bring a rake, so they used their fingers and hard twigs to clear rotting leaves and sturdy little vines from Daddy's grave, their fingers becoming muddy and scratched. Then Emory placed the tripod with the cross whose plaque read "Father. In loving memory" at the headstone and the wreath with blue flowers at the foot of the grave. Kate helped him, as always the Corliss women did their men, and as always, she thought she was being claimed by a part of her past that she had rejected. Nowadays, when away from her family, she lived a somewhat solitary life and mostly did things for herself. But when she was with them, she still reverted. Guiltily comforted by Emory's mastery of the situation, she watched his intent face as he carefully placed the thin wires into the muddy dirt. Not for the first time, she wondered what his relationship with their father had been. He had been spoiled, she knew, by both parents, as she herself had been in those first years before the others came, but, considering Mr. Corliss's uncertain temper, it must have been erratic nonetheless.

"I don't really like these flowers," she found herself saying in a rejection of old grief. Her youngest brother looked at her across a gulf and said, "We're doing this for Mom," at once apologetically as though he were not sure of her family solidarity and sympathetically as though he were in the same boat. Leaving behind their father—and Kate felt a wrench as though they were doing precisely that—they continued to the tiny grave of the stillborn twins. (Kate had been twelve when her mother started bleeding on the kitchen floor, when her father, white-faced and mute, rushed his wife to the hospital twenty miles away.) A dog barked frantically, and they looked to the house above and to the right of the graveyard, where yet another relative lived, although they did not know him. He had lived in Indiana most of his life since his parents had moved there seeking work, and now he had retired to live on his mother's old property. She was in a nursing home in Indiana. Kate remembered her older cousin, a pretty woman with a bleeding ear where her first husband had struck her. He had been an alcoholic, the family story went, but not a bad guy, except once in a while when he had been drinking for days.

Mamaw's grave was sunken and deep in rotting leaves. They scrabbled at the leaves, and Kate felt as though she were disturbing her grandmother's substance—not the older woman, thin and bent and sorrowful, but the younger, plump woman with red hair and enveloping arms who made the best chicken dumplings in the county, the family said, maybe in the state. For some years, between Kate's fourth and eighth years, long before Emory was born, she and her parents and the oldest two of the other siblings had lived in a medium-sized gray house in Osier County, on Sarvis Creek, a house with a large garden and a pasture and a creek and a cow, chickens, and a dog named Cricket. It had not been far from where she stood now. The place had been demolished by strip mining. But in those days, the graveyard was a mere whisper at the back of Kate's mind, and they would come weekly to Papaw and Mamaw's house. "She made the best chicken dumplings in the county," Kate said to her youngest brother in an elegiac tone. "I don't remember," he said regretfully.

By the time they had finished, it was after three, and Emory sounded rushed when he said, in his best organizational manner, "We'd better be getting on to Panther Fork," and, as he pulled out his cell phone, "I'll call Artie Gene." He had mentioned Artie Gene before; a cousin found as he did his genealogy researches, one of those familiar strangers he had called.

"Now, what's our relationship to Artie Gene," Kate said a little whimsically.

"He's Daddy's brother Matthew's grandson."

It was weird to be tutored by her brother, who, over the long years, had visited Kentucky only fleetingly and who now, going by their visit to Elsie and Bill, sounded more at home than she did.

So Emory called Artie Gene and had a genial man-to-man discussion about how to get to Panther Fork, which was near Sweet Branch. Kate was struck by the easy-sounding bonhomie in Emory's voice as he registered instructions from this stranger, not a word said about hail cousin, well met although both of them were now in their fifties and had never before laid eyes on each other.

Their parents had had their first home on Panther Fork, living for those first few years with *his* family, Kate suddenly thought and wondered why she had not had the thought before, or perhaps she had some time in the foggy past. They had left and gone to Mr. Corliss's dream state of Florida, and when they had come back, they had moved to Sarvis Creek, where Kate's memories were mostly of their mother's family. Kate had always seen her father, with his black hair and blue eyes and his kin living up hollers and his itchy foot, as poet and outsider. At the same time, he had been the breadwinner, the goer-out-into-the-world of their reclusive family. Nowadays, Kate also thought that their mother, by virtue of having lost the homeplace and Kentucky itself, was poetic in her reconstructions of and sense of loss about not only her childhood but also her young adult life—her early marriage to a man she had loved in the years before life bent him into an unhappy, often irascible partner.

Looking over at her brother as they got lost on their way to Artie Gene's, traveling through the clearing day, deeper into blue-sky-and-green-hills, Kate was sure that Emory, with all this genealogy, felt something akin to her own family enchantment, as did the rest of the family, cast out into the world—as, surely, most human families did on some level, even those of the illusory well-adjusted mainstream, because after all, everybody lost their childhood. What was it a mentor at the magazine in New York had said? "They took you away from that little farm in Kentucky and made a writer of you." He would probably be surprised to know that of all his words and advice; it was this pronouncement that she remembered most.

"Are you going to write a book out of all your discoveries," she asked her brother.

He said, sounding uncertain, "I don't know yet. I've thought about it."

"Think of all the family members who would buy it. *I* would buy it, that's for sure. And there's a lot of us," she said lightly, but she did not feel whimsical but enthusiastic and at the same time envious. Emory had been sending his siblings e-mails with little family stories reaching back to the fourteenth century. She already planned to use at least one of these stories as the basis of a short story.

"Look at that sign," he said. "This can't be right. We're almost in another county."

"Lost!"

"Not lost," her brother said. "We just overshot the mark, I think. Never say lost." He pulled out his cell phone and called Artie Gene, whom Kate was beginning to distrust as a leader down garden paths. "Okay," Emory was saying bluffly. "I see what we did wrong. Thanks, Artie." He turned his head toward Kate and said, half-joking, "Don't you tell anyone we got lost. We just went a little too far."

"A *little* too far? Okay, if you say so," she responded, half-teasing. His insistence was, she thought, partly a male role but partly too a desire not to be lost. She also did not want to be lost. They backtracked, swung onto Copper Road, but this time instead of going right and across the railroad tracks, they continued along the hillside that Kate had seen from the graveyard. The last time she had been here, this road had been under construction. She saw from its distance sights that seemed familiar but that were too distant both in space and time to be able to satisfy her nostalgia. A crucial nostalgia, she thought—not seeking the past's perfume but its very structure.

Then the Google map she was holding told them to turn left, and they did, onto a road that Google gave a name but which had no sign. It was a rougher road, and before too long, they were going across a small mountain on a one-lane road functioning as a two-lane road. Kate looked over the side at a narrow valley far below them. "This is supposed to be High View Road," she said wryly. He grimaced a little and replied firmly, "We won't come back this way."

Then they found themselves on Panther Fork, and Kate sighed with relief. Panther Fork's road was full of potholes. Emory stopped beside a small, neatly kept house with crocuses blooming all around. An old man, Kate found herself thinking as though she herself probably did not match his age, was bent over a lawnmower. Emory punched a button to roll down the windows and asked, "Are we on the right track for Corliss Lane?"

The old man straightened up to the best of his ability and replied politely but with no warmth, "I reckon you are. Just go on about a half-mile and you'll find it." He returned to his lawn mowing without further ado. Kate wondered if he had outlived curiosity or if the traffic on this road frequently spewed out lost tourists. She felt an impulse to talk to him, to ask him how long he had lived in the house, to ask him who he knew. Emory shook his head a little forlornly and pulled away.

And there it was, Corliss Lane, a short, neat, graveled path with a neat new sign. She wondered who had given the path its name and its gravel and how recently. It led first to Uncle Matthew's place, which she remembered, and then to a semicircle of three small houses. Between Matthew's house and the semicircle, there was a large garden, its spring plowing done. A man was bent above a large bed of lettuce and green onions. He looked shabby and ill-kempt. "I bet that's Artie Gene," Emory said dubiously. Instead of rolling down the windows, he got out, speaking to the man as he did so, "Artie?"

"That I am." Kate could see then that their cousin was emaciated, his clothes looking as though they had been borrowed from a robust brother. She thought of Elsie. "I see you're looking at Grandpa's house," he said to Emory, who replied, "I sure am. I remember coming here. This is Kate, my sister."

Artie said to her, "Well, come on out and make yourself at home." About Emory's age, he looked like his grandfather, Matthew, and spoke to them familiarly, as though in some sense they all belonged to each other. Emory was already walking around Uncle Matthew's house, which was plainly not occupied. "It's smaller than I remember," he said. Kate brought up from memory the last time she had seen her uncle and his wife, Selena. They had come out onto the shady porch, and Kate had been struck anew by her uncle's resemblance to her father—though his black hair was gray and his face longer than his brother's. There were the same deep-set blue eyes examining the world at moments as though it were an old and dubious proposition.

"Well, it's all that junk on the porch," their cousin was

saying. "I keep telling Carl—he's the one that owns it now—that he ought to clear it off." His older brother Carl lived in Michigan, where he had worked in a Ford plant before retiring. "He gets down here ever chance he has. If it wasn't for his kids and grandkids, he'd be living down here." Kate mentioned the little girl she had seen with Matthew and Selena. "Did Janie May make it all right?" she asked. From something she had heard from Aunt Selena on one of their visits home, she thought that the beautiful child was mentally retarded.

"Janie's doing fine," Artie said. "Married and the mother of five kids."

Emory said, "You got some nice peas about ready to blossom. I planted some in my backyard the other day. Got any special instructions?"

"Well, I leave it mostly to nature," Artie drawled. "Keep the weeds away and the hoe at hand and some water when it's necessary."

"I guess we'd better be getting along," Emory said, looking at Kate.

"You'll never git up to the graveyard in your car," Artie told him, and then as if it were an everyday occurrence, "I'll just take you in my pickup here."

Both the men seemed to think that Kate belonged in the middle of the narrow cab, her feet on the hillock in the center, knees rising up to meet her chin, paper flowers obstructing her view of the road. She was nervous as Artie Gene started the engine, but he seemed to have no trouble negotiating his driving in the crowded cab. Emory asked him if Aunt Selena was still alive. "Buried over on Rellard Hill, with Grandpa." "What about your Aunt Glesson? Where does she live now?" Artie answered with the sense of importance with which Emory spoke. He then treated

Emory to a history of the pickup and how handy it was.

They went a mile or so and then started climbing up a narrow, damaged blacktop. "If we meet somebody, they'll just have to do the backing up," Artie said. "I can't manage it with this truck." Mercifully, they made it to a shoulder broad enough to hold the truck, and Artie said, "From here on, we have to climb on foot." There was hardly a path through last year's dead leaves up up up on an incline so steep that Kate half-lost her footing and almost knocked Artie Gene back down the hill. She heard his breathing, so labored, more labored than her seventy years' wind, though he was almost twenty years younger.

They reached the graveyard. Graves scattered about, mostly simple but here and there beneath the sparse canopy of tall trees an elaborate headstone.

"This cemetery is still in use," Emory said with surprise, pointing to a fresh grave.

"We buried Ruth McCoy there two weeks ago. I helped carry up the casket," Artie said, looking at Kate. "You remember her? Second cousin. Jack McCoy's daughter." Kate shook her head, and Emory said, "Any relation to *the* McCoys?" There was a family rumor that on their father's side, they were related to the McCoys of the Hatfield-McCoy feud. Emory had pretty much scotched the rumor, but there was always a chance.

"Naaah. At least none that I know of," Artie replied. "I had trouble bringing her coffin up. Got this tumor in my lungs. Got to go start getting it burned out next week." He imparted this news casually, as though it were an everyday affair. Emory and Kate gave each other a significant look, and Emory said awkwardly, "Well, good luck with that." Kate added a silly, fervent "Yes," and the subject was put aside when Artie said, "That was some ginseng over there in the corner. We dug it up and dumped it. Didn't seem right to profit from it. It was beginning to wreck that old grave. Here's great-grandpa and grandma."

Still labored from the climb, struck by Artie's revelation that he had serious cancer, Kate looked down at her father's grandparents' graves, thinking of the picture hanging in the hall of the Corliss house: their great-grandfather had a long white beard and a solemn face, and his wife, also expressionless, wore a long black dress and had her hair pulled back in a bun. They were surrounded stiffly by eight of their children, posed in an unnatural manner. Probably an itinerant photographer had gathered them thus. Emory bent and began raking leaves away with his fingers. Kate joined him, feeling at a distressing remove from her past. She noted how tenderly her brother raked the graves and righted his great-grandmother's headstone.

"Over here," Artie said and pointed downward. There were the graves of their mother's dead children. One of them had lived long enough to be named. Garnet. Garnet Corliss, whose embroidered quilt, a creek meandering across it, bordered by willow trees, pale greens and pinks, made in anticipation by their mother, never used for her living children, was stored away in Mamaw's old trunk up in the attic. Kate had once written a poem about her, but now the shock of the day was too much, and she could only look down at the tiny grave and think here were more leaves to be raked. She watched Emory for a moment; his face closed as he attacked the problem with dedication.

It was only on their way back down the steep hill that Kate felt for her young mother, taken away from her family by this older man who had probably swept her off her feet, as a romance novel would put it, but which must have been much more complicated in the reality. Put down here in these strange hills amid his family and giving birth to dead babies. She said something along these lines to Emory, and he said, "Yes. I was thinking about it too." This was after they had left Artie Gene behind, thanking him, wishing him well on his upcoming treatment, looking at his neat and well-tended garden and at Uncle Matthew's junky porch. "You'll keep in touch with him?" she asked her brother. "He'd take it better coming from you." "Yes," Emory said shortly. Kate wondered if she were just passing the responsibility to him. She could tell from her brother's very brevity that he was undergoing an upheaval. Their father, too, had become wordless in the face of strong emotions. Most of his children, including Kate, had put on the mantle of this discretion to some degree. She thought of her young, voluble mother with that taciturn young man who grieved for his lost children in silence.

"How are the boys?" she asked.

"Scott is fine. Robert has developed complications from the flu. Looks like he's going to miss graduation," her brother answered somberly.

Why on earth hadn't he mentioned this earlier Kate asked herself. Their mother had told Kate about the flu, but she obviously didn't know about the "complications." How like Emory to keep the news to himself, she thought with affectionate exasperation. "What kind of complications?" she persisted.

"Bronchial problems. They're having trouble clearing up his chest," he said shortly and changed the subject. "Who should we visit first tomorrow?"

It was growing dark outside. Inside the closed car, Kate imagined the sound of tree frogs outside, the call of an owl, sitting on a long-dead aunt's porch and listening as she had done many years ago. Long before the man behind the steering wheel had been born. "Let's think about it after dinner," she said. "I just realized we skipped lunch." It was an easy family segue away from pain, and he accepted it naturally, saying, "Where are we going to eat?"

"Everything will be closed," she said comically. "It's Sunday evening in Osier County, and it's Easter on top of that."

They made their way to the hotel, that halfway house between the world they were used to and the one that was now claiming them. Tomorrow they would visit more kinfolk, a cousin who was a devout Baptist and the operator of a small mine, his sister in a nursing home, a long-married cousin who had allowed the child Kate to tag along after her (now suffering from Parkinson's), and an uncle known for his silent dignity and innate sweetness (about to die because of a heart condition) and his cheerful daughter the dentist— the people remaining whom Kate remembered most, with whom, when she was at her mother's, she sometimes spoke on the phone. Good will on both sides would carry the conversation for five minutes or so, and then she would hand the phone back to her mother, where the conversation might last for a half-hour to an hour as Mrs. Corliss and her phone companion would tell each other about the things that mattered. All of them still lived up hollers or in Copper, which no longer had its general store and post office and where passenger trains no longer stopped. Nowadays, they did most of their shopping at a chain supermarket outside Osierville. (There was no room for everything in town, squeezed as it was between mountains.) Emory and Kate passed a hardware store, a butcher shop, paint shop, cell phone vendor, furniture store, fast-food restaurant strung along U.S. 23, each isolated structure awkwardly disturbing a greening hillside as the growing town spilled out of its boundaries.

Out of the lovely dark into the brittle yet welcoming light of the hotel, they asked one of the busy people at the desk, a young man who might just have graduated from the university and been unable to find other work without leaving home, about a place to have dinner, and he told them that their best if not only bet was a bar down a block and around the corner. Back out into the slow sweet dark. The bar, on the first floor of a plain two-story brick building, was surprisingly discreet, announced only by a small glowing sign and the faint sound of music. Inside it might have been an upscale bar anywhere in the nation, excepting the pleasant drawl and twang of hill voices, and these were interspersed here and there by voices from elsewhere.

A blond girl dressed in jeans and a blue and green silk top guided them to an elevated booth away from the noise of the bar. "I think we've actually found a local hangout," Emory said in a pleased voice. "I don't see any college students, except maybe that table over in the corner." Kate ordered a po'boy and a glass of chardonnay, Emory a Reuben and a beer. As they waited for their food, they talked about Elsie and Artie Gene. "You know Elsie would still look good if she fixed herself up," Emory said dispassionately.

Looking at a mental picture of their cousin, Kate saw that he was right. She replied, echoing a black friend of her college days, "And Artie looks like death on a cracker, but you can see he once was a good-looking man." She thought about tomorrow and wondered what unhappy changes she might find, and she thought about how this encroaching age and sickness must strike her brother, who had not known these people in their heyday.

Their food came, and they changed the subject, commenting on the excellence of the po'boy and Reuben, munching hungrily. Suddenly Emory said, "His doctor says Robert's respiratory system is weak, and he isn't responding to the medicine as well as we would like. I haven't told Mom because she would worry too much."

"Is he in a hospital, Emory?"

"No, not now. He's back home, and he *is* getting better. Eileen is taking off some time from work while I do my gallivanting around. When I called last night, she said he had been on the phone with his friends for hours, which is a good sign. This Reuben is great. I could almost order another one."

Kate regarded her youngest brother as he bent his big, blunt head over his plate. On a wave of affection and respect, she almost said, "What if I came down to visit in the fall?" But then she thought of his current trouble and his treasured reticence and refrained. Perhaps next year would be better. The chasm of absent years, of different worlds and commitments, of age, was there, but they had made contact, and that would do for now. Her brother mentioned a man he had run across doing his research who had married three wives between 1915 and 1918, one of them a great-aunt who seemed to have disappeared in thin air. Emory had spent a good deal of time trying to track her down. They sipped their drinks in the lively enclave set down in the middle of childhood, surrounded by the great dark hills.

Acknowledgments

First I must thank Penelope Fanning, without whose encouragement and generosity over the years these stories might have been stillborn, or at best in a file drawer somewhere. Corrine Falope also has provided help and inspiration since our college days. And how not to thank my many siblings, with special thanks to Sonia and Danny, who add meaning to my life on a daily basis? There are so many more in so many places that I owe thanks to. I hope those still among the living will consider it said. I have been blessed.

"Going Home" appeared years ago, in an earlier, quite different version, as "The Old Woman," in the Ohio Wesleyan *Owl*.

About Atmosphere Press

Atmosphere Press is an independent, full-service publisher for excellent books in all genres and for all audiences. Learn more about what we do at atmospherepress.com.

We encourage you to check out some of Atmosphere's latest releases, which are available at Amazon.com and via order from your local bookstore:

Facehash, a novel by Reuben Percival

The You I See, a novel by Danny Freeman

Neanderthal Gita, a novel by Michael Baldwin\

Tsunami, a novel by Paul Flentge

Donkey Show, a novel by Stephen Baker

Take a Bow: An American in Tokyo, a novel by T. Stonefield

Original Mind Disconnect, a novel by Michael R. Bailey

Paper Targets, a novel by Patricia Watts

Don't Poke the Bear, a novel by Robin D'Amato

Tubes, a novel by Penny Skillman

Skylark Dancing, a novel by Olivia Godat

ALT, a novel by Aleksandar Nedeljkovic

The Bonds Between Us, a novel by Emily Ruhl

Dancing with David, a novel by Siegfried Johnson

The Friendship Quilts, a novel by June Calender

My Significant Nobody, a novel by Stevie D. Parker

Nine Days, a novel by Judy Lannon

About the Author

Jo Ann Kiser is a native of the eastern Kentucky hills whom chance has allowed a rich and varied life, from her childhood in the hills, to being a "checker" at The New Yorker, to completing a dissertation on Proust at the University of Chicago. She has also taught briefly at Morehead State University in Kentucky and at Tennessee Tech. *The Guitar Player and Other Songs of Exile* is her first full-length work to be published.

Photograph by Kelly Lyle

Made in the USA
Monee, IL
20 November 2022

17947699R00142